Dreams

Marie Satterwhite

authorHOUSE®

AuthorHouse™
1663 Liberty Drive
Bloomington, IN 47403
www.authorhouse.com
Phone: 1 (800) 839-8640

Published by AuthorHouse 08/24/2016

ISBN: 978-1-5246-2246-6 (sc)
ISBN: 978-1-5246-2244-2 (hc)
ISBN: 978-1-5246-2245-9 (e)

Library of Congress Control Number: 2016912742

Print information available on the last page.

Acknowledgements

To Kathy Soltic, a woman I found online, who took out the time to read over my material and help me with editing. She motivated me with her soft spoken words and encouraged me by affirming that I could write a good novel.

I would also like to thank God for my co-worker and friend, Valerie Cater for introducing me to two (2) very special people. Those people are my ghostwriter and editor, Deborah McDaniel and my graphic design artist, Duvall Brown. Valerie and I shared a lot of long lunches constantly discussing this novel, and I guess she said, "Let me get this girl some help!" Thank you so much, Valerie. I love you!

Also, I thank my beautiful niece, Chakhan Dews. She brought the cover to life with her beauty and by being so photogenic. You go, Girl! I love you.

She must have come from heaven as an angel with her writing and editing skills, hard work, and patience because she helped me bring this novel, Dreams to a reality. Deborah McDaniel is truly a professional woman, writer and editor. I am truly blessed to have had her as my editor on my lifetime project. Thank you, my friend.

Duvall Brown, my graphic design artist, worked his magic and created a deeply intense cover just from a conversation with me. He took what I said and ran with it. Thank you very much for taking the time and having the patience to work with me.

And to the man behind the scene my marketer Tone Frie. I started running before the gun was shot, so now I'm walking back with my head down. So go on and run with it dog, take the wheel Tone take the wheel.

I would like to thank my family and friends for all of their support. I love you all!

And last, but most importantly, I would like to thank You, Lord for all these wonderful people that You brought into my life. AMEN!

Dedication

To God, for giving me the energy to pursue this dream of writing a novel. Lord, I give You all the praise and the glory!

To Linda Smith, who was there from the beginning of my writing this novel, listening to all of my late night rantings. Look, Girl! Dreams is a reality now.

To the memory of Betty Arnold, my mother, who believed in me, but would often say that I would never get this novel published because I'm always messing around. Look, Mom! I'm not dragging my feet anymore. You are truly missed. I love you, Mom.

To the memory of Calvin Paige, the love of my life, who would always laugh and tease me saying, "How long have you been writing this novel?" Look, Honey! I'm done!

To my children, Arthur and Shiena Satterwhite, growing up and making me think that they were listening to me talking about this novel, but I'm sure they were ignoring me. It's not over yet. Another novel is coming!

1

After driving around for more than an hour, even though her commute from the Brown Bag Delicatessen, should have only taken fifteen minutes, she couldn't stop thinking about her experience at the restaurant. Kim Nelson looked at the clock on the dashboard of her red 2013 Nissan Maxima with black leather interior, and saw that it was 7:30 p.m. on this blistery, cold first Friday in February. She pulled into the parking lot of her apartment complex on South High Street on the Southside of Columbus, Ohio. The aroma of her corned beef sandwich and fries filled the car and almost distracted her from the pain and anguish she felt after what she'd just experienced.

She checked her rear view mirror as she prepared to back into her parking space and noticed how red and puffy her eyes were from crying. Once she had parked, she couldn't bring herself to get out of the car. So, she just sat there. Everything was quiet and calm, which contrasted with the turmoil that went on inside her mind and heart. And even though the night seemed darker than usual, the parking lot was well lit. She turned off the car engine, and after sitting for a moment, she looked over at the passenger seat at her dinner, and before she knew it, she was hitting the Styrofoam container until pieces of meat from her sandwich started to emerge from the sides of the box. She looked around to see if anyone had witnessed her tantrum, but she was alone in the parking lot. She reached for her purse and placed her hand on the lever to open her car door. Len suddenly appeared at her side. Immediately, she locked the doors.

"Go away, Len," she shouted.

His deep brown eyes peered in at her with intense desperation, but she refused to let them convince her. She couldn't deal with him right now. He banged on the window as if his life depended upon getting her to respond to him.

"I just want to talk to you, Kim. Open the door!"

"No!" she yelled. She turned on the radio. Her favorite station was Magic 95.5 FM they played R&B classics and hits. She turned the volume up so loud that it penetrated her closed window and thundered throughout the parking lot, drowning out Len's pleas for her to talk to him.

His banging and pleading joined with the loud music pierced through the windows of the car as well as the windows of the residents' apartments.

Kim could see her neighbors' lights coming on, curtains being pulled back, as well as blinds and windows opening. She knew that it was only a matter of time before someone called the police, but Len didn't seem to notice as he continued banging, the glass vibrating under the force of his fist.

After a few minutes, she heard police sirens. She cracked her window and said "you better leave! Someone has called the police," she warned Len. Suddenly, the sound of shattering glass startled her as the car window gave way from Len's constant pounding. Kim blocked her face from the rain of glass with her arm, but she felt a sharp pain on her side. When she took her arm away from her face, she saw Len being tackled to the ground by a police officer. The cop his knee in Len's back as he placed him in handcuffs. She unlocked the door, and another officer opened it.

"Are you okay?" he asked.

Before she could answer, she saw blood on the side of her white blouse, dripping onto her red skirt. She had taken her coat off when she got into the car. The officer followed her eyes to the blood stain, and told his partner to call for an ambulance. As the other officer headed back to their vehicle with Len in cuffs, Kim could still hearing Len yelling.

"I just came over to talk! She knows that I would never hurt her! Kim, are you alright?"

Kim reached for her coat, put it around her shoulders and got out of the car. Now, she could feel blood running down her side. When she looked into the officer's eyes, she realized that they knew each other.

"Kim?" he questioned. "What's going on?"

"Nothing, Sam. He wasn't trying to hurt me. He just wanted to talk, and I kept ignoring him, so he kept banging on the window in order to get my attention. The broken glass was an accident. I don't need to press charges or anything."

"Well, even though I don't think it's wise for you not to press charges, I respect your decision. But, you need to see a doctor. An ambulance is on the way. In the meantime, we'll request for a constant patrol of this lot until you have a chance to fix your window. I'll put some plastic up to it for now and meet you at the hospital to take your statement."

"Thanks, Sam," Kim told him. Moments later, the ambulance arrived, and the paramedics jumped out and rushed toward her.

2

When Kim arrived at Riverside Hospital, she was transported into an examination room where she waited to see a doctor. A nurse had come in to clean and bandage her wound. Then, the nurse informed her that she might need stitches so she had to wait for a doctor to see her before she could be released. As she lay there on the examination table, she thought about how much her life had changed within a matter of hours.

Until just a few hours ago, she thought she had a good life, loving family, good job and a man who loved her with his whole heart and wanted to marry her. She didn't think she could ask for anything more. Nevertheless, she had to be honest with herself, she had been down this road many times before—many, many times before.

She went over the events in her mind. She had gotten off work early and missing Len because she knew they weren't going to be able to get together that evening, she decided to go to one of their favorite restaurants to pick up a bite to eat the Brown Bag Deli. She loved their corned beef sandwiches so she decided that she would pick up one to go and spend another Friday evening home watching television because Len always had to work late on Fridays.

She walked in smiling—the restaurant was always so warm and cozy, and the people were always so friendly. She knew every time she came in, she would be greeted like she was family. She sat at the bar instead of getting a seat in the dining room to place her order.

"Hey, lady, are you here alone today?" the server asked.

"Yes, he works on Friday evenings," Kim said.

"Well, what can I get for you?"

Kim ordered the corned beef sandwich that she'd been yearning for with a side of fries and decided to have a glass of wine while she waited for her order. Sipping on the wine, she let the soothing sounds of the soft music playing in the background bathe her soul as people talked quietly over their meals in the soft gold glow of the place. She heard a voice that sounded like Len's from a table on the other side of the bar.

"No, Baby. No ice cream until all your food is gone."

"Damn, I really must be missing this man," Kim said to herself.

Several minutes later, the server placed her order in front of her with the bill, and she heard the voice again:

"Good job! You ate all of your food. Now, you can have some ice cream."

She paid the bill with her credit/debit card, finished her wine, and prepared to leave. One of the servers approached her and said, "Hey, Girl! How are you this evening? Your husband and kids are at the table around the corner."

She looked at the server in total disbelief. Having to see for herself, she walked around the corner to the table, and there her man sat—with two young children, a boy and a girl! Before she could call his name, he saw her.

"Kim!" He got up from the table and walked over to her.

"Daddy, where are you going?" the little boy asked. He looked to be about five or six.

"Stay here," he told the little boy. "Eat your ice cream and watch your sister. I'll be right over here." The little girl looked to be about three or four years of age.

Kim turned and started to walk toward the door.

"Please don't walk out. I need to keep an eye on my children."

She turned back and walked over to him. "You're supposed to be at work, and here you are at a restaurant with some children that I never knew about! Why didn't you tell me about your children?" Kim asked. She was livid.

"I can explain that, but I can't do it right here—not right now. Can I come see you later?"

"No, tell me now! Are these your children?"

"Yes, of course, they're my children."

"Is there anything else I need to know?" Kim asked, looking down at the ring on the third finger of his left hand. "Funny. I never noticed you wearing that before!"

They were both speaking in hushed, urgent tones.

"Can we talk about this later?"

"No! I need to know right here and now."

He moved closer to her, and said, keeping the hushed, urgent tone, but sounding a bit more emphatic, "Yes, I'm married. But," he whispered even softer, "I am getting divorced soon."

Tears rolled down Kim's face, "I thought you loved me. You told me that you were already divorced, Len! You've just been lying to me, like every other man I've known! And, when were you going to tell me about the children? We've been dating for almost a year, and you let me think you were single with no children at all. You're just a liar!"

She pushed past him and headed for the door. She could hear his son ask, "Who is that lady, Daddy?" But what pierced her heart was his reply.

"Nobody, Son."

The tears rolled again as she lay back on the examination table, trying to push the memories out of her mind. Sam, the officer who had come to assist her with Len, entered the examination room. She had met him at her job as a legal secretary for Attorney Belinda T. Caldwell. He'd come to the office for several weeks to be deposed for a criminal trial. It was one of the few times a defense lawyer used a police officer as a witness for the defense. When Sam would come in, they would often engage in small talk while he waited in the reception area for Ms. Caldwell to see him. Sometimes, they even went to lunch together on the days when he had to spend several hours working on a deposition. They became good friends.

"Oh, there you are," he said as he approached. Obviously, noticing her tears, he hugged her. "You want to tell me what happened?"

"I just keep finding myself in these relationships with men who can't commit to me."

All of a sudden, she jumped up from the examination table and fell to her knees at a nearby wastebasket and began to vomit. Sam grabbed a washcloth from a cart in the hall, dampened it in the nearby sink, and used it to help Kim wipe her face.

"Thanks, Sam. Every time I think about what happened today, I get sick to my stomach."

Sam poured her a cup of water and handed it to her. "I know it's hard for you to talk about what happened, but I need a statement for my police report."

Kim took a few sips of the water to try to rid her tongue of the putrid taste of vomit "I pulled into my apartment parking lot, and before I knew what was happening, Len was standing there. He wanted to talk to me, but I refused, so he started to bang on the car window. I didn't think he was hitting it hard enough to cause it to break, but the next thing I knew, glass was everywhere, and here I am in the hospital waiting to be stitched up."

"What was so urgent he needed to speak with you about?"

"We got into an argument earlier this evening, and he wanted to discuss it some more, but I wasn't ready to talk."

"Is there anything else you would like to add to the statement?" Sam asked. His look of sincere concern touched Kim.

Before she could respond, a young, white doctor entered the room and introduced himself as Dr. Williams. Sam excused himself, saying he was going to a vending machine to get a snack for himself. "Do you want anything?" he asked Kim, but she shook her head to indicate she didn't. Dr. Williams removed the bandages that the nurse had applied to Kim's side to look at her wound.

"Well, Miss Nelson the cut doesn't look too bad. The bleeding has stopped, but you will need a few stitches."

"Will it leave a scar?"

"No. It shouldn't leave a scar. There is an ointment that I can prescribe for you that will ensure that your skin heals completely if that's a major concern for you. Let's get you stitched up, and you should be able to go home in an hour or so."

"Okay. Thanks."

When the doctor left the room, promising to be back in about ten minutes to stitch Kim's wound, Sam came back and sat at her side. He handed her a pack of peanut butter crackers. "Here, maybe this might help you with that nausea. You're not pregnant, are you?"

"No. Just upset," Kim felt it was a fair question. "Do you have everything you need for your report?" she asked.

"Yes, I just thought you might need someone to sit with you," he told her as he bit into a Snicker candy bar.

"That's nice of you," she told him as she rested the back of her head on the pillow and began to peel the wrapping off of the crackers. "The doctor said that it might take about an hour before I can leave."

"I can give you ride home," Sam offered.

"I'd appreciate that. I really don't want to have to tell anyone in my family about what happened tonight."

"Do you think that guy will be bothering you anymore?"

"Sam, he doesn't want to hurt me—at least not physically."

"I just want to make sure you're safe."

Kim looked at Sam. He was handsome for a white guy, she thought—blue eyes, sandy, curly short hair. He had a certain innocence in his countenance that warmed her heart. She knew he wanted to ask her out, but she always steered the conversation away from romance whenever she felt he was flirting. "I know you do," she told him.

Dr. Williams returned moments later, administered the stitching to her wound, signed her release papers, and gave her going home instructions with bandages and prescriptions for pain as well as the ointment he promised.

After escorting her to the hospital pharmacy to fill her prescriptions, Sam drove her home.

3

Kim was relieved to finally be home. She shed her clothing, put on her black silk pajamas, pulled her dark, wavy, shoulder-length hair up into a ponytail, and got into bed. She looked around at the gray walls of her room. Her décor was red, black and gray. Red was her favorite color. She admired the red lacquer armoire that stood proudly by her bed that showcased a black lacquer headboard. A black, red and gray comforter adorned with red throw pillows covered her queen-sized bed. Her sheets matched her black silk pajamas. She usually found such great comfort in the coziness of her bedroom, but tonight the reds only reminded her of the blood that she'd lost this evening. The blacks reminded her of the death of her relationship with Len, and the grays reminded her of how sad she felt inside that yet another relationship had come to its end. Loneliness overwhelmed her, and even though it was after midnight, she couldn't go to sleep.

Maybe she should have invited Sam in for a glass of wine. He would have loved that, she thought. Nevertheless, she knew that if she gave Sam the slightest bit of hope, she'd never be able to get rid of him. Why couldn't she like guys like Sam? The ones who actually would give anything to be with her. She knew Sam was single. That's all he could talk about when he would come to Atty. Caldwell's office—how he wished he could find the right woman!

She needed to talk to her best friend, Sheila who lived in Cleveland, Ohio. Sheila had originally lived in Columbus, and Kim had met her at South High School when they were in the 10ᵗʰ grade. They did everything together in high school. They scheduled their classes together. They ate lunch together. They spent the night at each other's homes. They even double-dated up until Sheila got married.

Sheila had met her husband, Damon, when Kim was in college at The Ohio State University. Sheila didn't want to go to college. She wanted to work in law enforcement. So instead of going to college, she took the civil service test and got a job with the Columbus Police Department in Dispatch not long after high school graduation.

Sheila would often visit Kim on campus for football and basketball games. Damon was in his last year at Ohio State when they met, and he was a Cleveland native. Once he graduated, he wanted to go back home to Cleveland, and he wanted Sheila to go with him. So, she packed up all her worldly possessions, put in for a transfer to the Cleveland Police Department, went to Cleveland with him and married him—much to the chagrin of her family. And, if the truth be told, Kim wasn't that happy about it either. Even though she loved Sheila, she always secretly resented her for leaving Columbus and for finding a husband before she did.

The clock read 1:30 a.m. when Kim picked up the phone to call Sheila. Kim knew it was a bit disrespectful to call a married woman at this time of night. Sheila and Damon could have been getting their freak on, and here she was calling to discuss her break up with Len. Well, Kim thought to herself, if they're having sex, shame on her if she answers the phone. The phone rang about six or seven times with no answer. Finally, she hung up.

Kim knew she should stop calling, but she felt desperate. She had to talk to somebody. She couldn't call her mother or her sister, Karen. Her mother couldn't even get a man since her father had died, and she should have let him go—the way he cheated on her throughout the years. And Karen acted like she was so into her career that men just weren't necessary. Kim didn't want to hear what they had to say, and to be honest, she was ashamed to tell them that she'd been cheated on once again. She got out of bed and began to pace the floor, occasionally looking out of the window of her apartment down to the parking lot where she could see her red Nissan Maxima that she adored with a big piece of ugly plastic taped to the driver's window.

She called Sheila again. This time the phone rang four times.

"Hello," Sheila said, sounding like she was still half asleep.

"He's married with two kids!" Kim told her, sobbing uncontrollably as she plopped down on the side of her bed and pulled tissue from its holder that sat perfectly on the red lacquer nightstand.

She continued to ramble on, but her words were virtually incomprehensible through her crying.

"Kim, please calm down! I can't understand anything you're saying." Sheila's tone was hushed. Kim assumed she was trying not to awake Damon.

Kim looked over her shoulder at the empty place in her bed next to where she sat. "How's Damon?" she asked.

"He's great, Kim. But, you didn't call to make small talk about my husband. Now, listen, are you going to be okay?"

"I don't know," she whispered through sobs. "I feel like my heart is breaking into a million pieces. Sheila, I'm so tired of men hurting me— lying to me!"

"Well, what happened this time?"

"I walked up on him in a restaurant with his two children, and he had on a wedding ring that I'd never even seen before!" The memory evoked so much pain that Kim could barely breathe.

"Listen, Kim. It's going to be okay. Tomorrow is Saturday. I will drive up first thing in the morning, and I'll help you get through this."

"I'm in so much pain, Sheila."

"Emotional or physical pain?"

"Both. Len followed me back to my apartment, and he started banging on my car window for me to open the door, and the window shattered. The glass hit me and I had to get stitches." She raised her pajama top to inspect the bandage. She grimaced at the sight of the blood that oozed through it.

"Glass? Oh my goodness, Kim. I'll be there by 8 or 9 in the morning. Will you be okay until then?"

"I don't know."

"Just get some sleep. By the time you wake up in the morning, I'll be there."

"I can't sleep."

"Okay, well put on some Maze. That's your favorite, and it's soothing. I'll stay on the phone with you until you fall asleep."

Kim picked up the remote control for her stereo from the nightstand and pressed play on her Maze playlist. "Time Is On My Side" played first as Sheila began to talk about her plans to buy something special this year for Damon on Valentine's Day.

Kim didn't really want to hear about Sheila and Damon's plans for Valentine's Day. It just made her feel worse about her own inability to find a husband. However, the soothing sounds of Maze and Sheila's rambling about her romantic plans bored her sufficiently to put her to sleep somewhere in the middle of "Happy Feelings."

4

Kim walked into an office with cherry oak wood furniture, gray walls with white trim, and gray carpet. She admired it for its contemporary look and feel. A man dressed in navy blue stood at a big window overlooking the city. He stared out at the city's skyline. Kim could tell that he was handsome from his build and his fresh haircut. His shoulders were broad. His stature was tall, but sturdy.

"Hello. I was told that I would find you here." She placed a stack of file folders on the desk.

"I've been waiting for you, Beautiful," he replied.

"I love this office," Kim told him as she turned her back to him to take it in. "And, you look so powerful standing there looking out over the city's skyline, but the feel of this office is so warm and welcoming." He approached her from behind and embraced her, squeezing her breasts gently.

She felt herself melt a little at his touch. He kissed her neck gently. "You're so beautiful," he whispered. "I love you."

"I love you, too."

He slid her black blazer off her shoulders and let it fall to the floor. He unzipped her red lace dress in the back as he kissed her neck and nibbled on her ears from behind.

"I want you right here," he whispered, breathing heavily.

"I want you, too," she whispered back.

He reached for the remote control to a black Bose stereo system located on a cherry oak wood bookcase. Kim's favorite song, "Happy Feelings," by Frankie Beverly and Maze emanated from the top notch speaker system with crystal clear sound. Then, he pushed files, pictures, papers and everything off the desk, took off his jacket, and laid it down for Kim as he gently leaned her over the desk, while kissing her softly on her back. Then, he resumed nibbling her earlobe, sucking it as if it were a watermelon Jolly Rancher—only stopping to slide her red panties from around her hips, past her thighs, her legs and her feet where she stepped out of them moments after her blazer, dress and bra hit the floor.

"Your skin is so soft." He panted with desire.

"Your hands are so magical." She immersed herself in the gentleness of his touch. "What if someone comes in?"

"You're going to be my wife," he whispered. "I'm sure they will understand how much we love and want each other."

She heard him unzip his pants, and she felt the pants hit the floor. She wanted to turn around to face him, but he resisted her. Then, he began to penetrate her gently inch by inch. She took in deep breaths, trying to absorb all of him. He filled up every inch of her being, and he stroked her gently, and he felt better than any man she'd ever had made love with before.

"You like that?" he asked in a soft tone.

"I love it," she said, moaning.

"Can you take it all?"

"I can."

He began to move rhythmically and gently, giving her more pleasure than she ever thought possible. He told her that he loved her over and over again. She had waited her whole life for a man to talk to her like this, make love to her like this, and commit to her like this. As she screamed with ecstasy, she awakened to realize that it was a dream, and that she was pleasuring herself.

She was drenched with sweat. She looked at the clock on her nightstand. It read 5:30 a.m. Her music was still on in the back ground. Bobby Bland's "Member Only" was playing. Thoughts of Len returned—seeing him in the restaurant with his children. Answering his son, "Nobody." Her high school sweetheart that she gave her virginity to on prom night, saying that he was in love with someone else. Gerald, the guy she dated a couple of years ago, confessing when he was caught lying that he was living with another woman. Jimmy, the guy she dated in college, who had his true love back home in Cincinnati, Ohio.

The memories of all her failed relationships with men who were already committed to someone else and could not or would not commit to her came rushing into her thoughts and her heart like a herd of stallions, stampeding on her soul, her hopes, her dreams. She didn't think she would ever experience the love of a man like she'd just had in that dream. No one had ever loved her anything close to that, but it was what she wanted most in the world. She didn't think she could face another day knowing that she would never know that kind of love. She longed for it with everything in her. The love that she had just experienced in her dream seemed so real, but deep inside she knew it was a love that she would never experience in reality.

The pain in her heart and soul gave way to physical pain. Her side where she had received the stitches throbbed. She picked up the bottle of prescription pain pills from the night stand. The directions said to take one pill every four hours with food. She went to the kitchen to get water. She returned to her bedroom and sat on the bed. She poured the contents of the pill bottle on her nightstand and absently, she put one pill after another in her mouth, using the water to help her swallow. After several minutes, she had consumed the whole bottle. The pain started to go away and she started to feel sleepy again. She lay down on her bed listening to Bobby Bland's "You've Got to Hurt Before You Heal" as she drifted back into a deep, soothing sleep.

5

⚭

When Kim awoke, she was in a bed at the hospital. Her vision was blurry at first, but once she began to focus, she saw Sheila sitting in a chair nearby.

"What happened?" she asked Sheila.

Sheila jumped up from her seat. "Hey! You're awake. Thank God!"

"Where am I?"

"I brought you to Riverside. Did you take all those pills on purpose?"

"What?"

"Do you want me to call your mother?"

Kim's memory started to return. She remembered taking the pills. She remembered the dream. She remembered Len in the restaurant. She remembered his words, "Nobody, Son." She remembered the shattering glass. She remembered the stitches in her side, but she didn't feel much pain.

"No! Don't call my mother. I don't want her to know what's going on. What time is it? What day is it?"

"It's Saturday morning," Sheila stated. She was obviously upset. She took a quick glance at her watch. "It's 11 o'clock. Kim, what *is* going on?" Sheila barked the question. "Did you try to kill yourself?"

"Of course, not," Kim replied and turned her back to Sheila, trying to avoid her eyes, but also trying to find a comfortable position.

"Don't you dare lie to me Kim Nelson! We're better than that. I didn't drive two and half hours to play games with you. You better tell me what's going on with you, and you better tell me right now! They have you in the psychiatric ward, Girl! On round the clock watch-care!"

Kim still didn't face Sheila. Tears began to stream down her face once again. "Okay, you're right. I tried to commit suicide."

"Why would you do that, Kim?" Sheila's voice was so urgent, it frightened Kim.

"I just don't want to live like this anymore, Sheila. I want a husband like you. I want to be loved. I'm lonely. I'm miserable."

"Kim, the right man is going to come along. You just have to be a little more patient, and stop…" Sheila stopped short of finishing her remark.

Kim raised her head and turned to face her friend. "Stop what?" she asked.

"Kim, we can talk about this later. They want you to talk to a counselor or a therapist to see if it's okay for you to be released."

"Being released from this hospital is starting to become a routine for me. I was just here last night." Kim said as she sat up straight in the bed and looked around.

"What are you looking for?" Sheila asked.

"I want something to drink."

Sheila stepped into the bathroom and grabbed a water pitcher and a glass. She filled the pitcher with water and brought it out, placing the pitcher on the nightstand by Kim's hospital bed after she poured a cup of water. "Here you go," she said as she handed Kim the glass.

"Thanks. So, do you have any idea when I will be seeing this therapist?"

Sheila sat in the chair again. "A nurse came by just before you woke up and said it should be within the hour."

"Len really hurt me, Sheila. He's married. He has two children. I can't believe I keep falling for these guys who keep lying to me. Men, who are already in relationships with other women."

"Kim, maybe you need a change of pace. You ever considered relocating?"

"Relocating?"

"Yes, I would love it if you moved to Cleveland. Maybe, you just need a change of scenery—a new pool of men. Hell, I think I might even be able to set you up on a date or two. I know plenty of men with the Cleveland Police Department who are single and looking, and Damon has a few single friends, too."

Kim perked up. "That's sounds great, Sheila. But, what about a job?"

"Are you kidding?" Sheila waved her hand in a gesture that said, 'piece of cake!' "Girl, you're a legal secretary. With your legal background and experience, the Cleveland Police Department would be a perfect place for you to continue your career. I'll start looking for openings as soon as I go back to work on Monday. I'll find you some jobs to apply for in no time! In the meantime, make sure that you make arrangements to take the civil service exam."

"I will. We have a test coming up in the next couple of weeks. You're such a great friend, Sheila. I don't know what I'd do without you."

"Well, thank God, you'll never have to find out, and I don't know what I'd do without you. So, no more of this taking pills trying to take yourself out!"

They smiled warmly at each other just as a woman in a white lab coat that covered a black suit entered the room. She was white with short, black hair, and a little bit too much red lipstick.

"Well, it's good to see the patient is in good spirits after your ordeal," she said, checking notes on some papers that were attached to a clipboard. "How are you feeling, Ms. Nelson?"

"I'm much better. Thank you."

"I need to talk to you privately if your friend doesn't mind," the woman told Kim and Sheila. "My name is Dr. Lynn Stevens, and I will be making the decision as to whether you're okay to be released."

"Kim, I have to go call Damon. I'll be right back," Sheila said getting up from her seat.

"Okay," Kim told her as she left the room.

Dr. Stevens watched Sheila as she exited and closed the door behind her. Then, she took a seat where Sheila had just gotten up.

"Now that we're alone. How are you really doing, Ms. Nelson?" She clicked her pen in a gesture that told Kim that she was prepared to take notes on whatever response she gave her.

"I'm fine," Kim stated.

"Ms. Nelson, you took about thirty prescription strength pain killers last night. I don't think you're fine. If your friend had not come to visit you this morning, you would be dead. Do you realize that? Is that what you wanted? Did you want to commit suicide? Or did you somehow take over thirty pain killers accidentally?"

"I was depressed. I experienced a traumatic event last night. I have seven stitches on my side! Did you see them?"

"Yes, Ms. Nelson. I'm aware that you were seen here last night for a serious cut wound, but I can't let you go home if you're a danger to yourself."

"I overreacted to a break up with my boyfriend. I'm okay now. I'm glad I didn't kill myself."

"That's good. And if you ever feel like that again, you have to remember that if you just give things a little more time, you will be glad that you're still alive. No matter how bad things get, they always get better, eventually." She pulled a card from her lab coat pocket. "Here, you can use this card if you need to. It's the number to the suicide hotline."

"It's just that I've been struggling with this same problem all my life. It seemed hopeless. But my friend just offered me a suggestion that gave me hope." Kim took the card and stared at it for a few moments before she laid it on the nightstand.

"Oh, that's good. What was her suggestion?"

"She thinks I should relocate to Cleveland, Ohio."

"A change of scenery has been known to help many people get a new perspective on life, but I think you need some outpatient care. Would you be willing to meet with me once a week for counseling?"

"I suppose I could, but I want to move to Cleveland as soon as I find a job. So then what?"

"I could recommend a therapist in Cleveland. Nevertheless, before I sign release papers for you today, I want your consent for outpatient treatment."

"Okay," Kim told Dr. Stevens just as Sheila opened the door and peeped in to see if she could come back.

"I'm done with Ms. Nelson. Come on in," she told Sheila. "I'll bring the forms back for you to sign once I get one of the nurses to print out your home going instructions. Is that okay?"

"That's fine," Kim replied.

6

When Richard Kemper burst into Lisa Brown's office on the first Monday morning in May, he had total disregard for the fact that she was interviewing a female applicant. He looked like he had been working harder than a Hebrew slave. The sleeves of his light blue shirt were rolled up, and he had obviously shed the suit jacket that matched the navy blue slacks he wore. A light mist of sweat adorned his forehead.

"So, what are your short-term goals?" he heard her ask.

"I just wanna be able to take care of me and my baby until my baby's daddy gets out of jail," was the young lady's reply, while tapping the top of her head. Richard hoped she was trying to knock some sense into it.

"Listen, Lisa," he said, chuckling to himself as he watched the head of Human Resources struggle to keep a dignified look on her face after hearing the applicant's response to her question. "When are you going to hire a secretary for me?"

"Ms. Peterson, could you excuse us for a moment. I need to have a brief discussion with Lieutenant Kemper, and then, we can finish this interview."

"Well, do you know how long you gonna be? I left Tykwan with my mama, and she said she got somewhere to go."

"We won't be long, Ms. Peterson. Give me about ten minutes."

The young lady twirled a curl at the end of her shoulder length hair weave, popped her gum three times in quick succession, and jumped up from her seat. Richard smirked as he observed her attire—a bright yellow form-fitting knit dress that came too much above her knees and revealed way too much cleavage to be appropriate for a job interview, but might work very nicely for a night club. She headed to the reception area outside of Lisa Brown's office, and he took her seat.

"Well, that was rude!" Lisa said.

"I know. How she gonna dispute your request for her to leave your office, and she's trying to get you to hire her? The nerve of some people!" Richard crossed his leg and reared back in the chair. He wiped his brow in anticipation of what he hoped would be a productive conversation between him and Lisa.

"I wasn't referring to her, Lieutenant Kemper. How dare you interrupt me when I'm in the middle of an interview!"

"Is that what that was?" Richard laughed and began to rifle through the file folders on Lisa's desk. "Look, I apologize for the interruption, but I need a new secretary like yesterday."

Lisa snatched the file folders from him and placed them on the computer desk behind her. Her extension braids swung as she swiveled her chair around. "I was interviewing that young lady to *be* your secretary," Lisa told him. Her smooth, chocolate face seemed to glisten a bit as Richard appraised her almost unconsciously. Lately, he had found himself analyzing and assessing every attractive woman he encountered, which was unusual for him. He normally only had eyes for his wife, Janice.

"The hell you preach!" Richard shouted. "I know you weren't planning to hire her for *me*. I need someone competent, and you know it!"

Lisa laughed. "I'm just messing with you, and you deserve it for being so rude. I'm on it, but there have been virtually no qualified applicants to interview. However, the results from the last civil service exam are in. It might provide some good prospects."

Lisa's phone rang. She picked it up. While waiting for her to finish the call, Richard observed Lisa's office, looking for some clues that might indicate that she was doing all she could to find a secretary for him. As the lead detective of the Cleveland Police Department's homicide unit, he was trained to look for clues and evidence. After over fifteen years in law enforcement, it was second nature to him.

The walls in her office were a pale yellow, and they were adorned with Black art, that had purposely themed splashes of red in every picture. Some of the pictures featured historical figures such as Malcolm X, Dr. King, African kings and queens. She had an L-shaped desk with light wood finish and black fabric chairs—one for her; two for guests, and alongside the wall at her office's entrance was a black leather sofa. About four African violets lined the cabinet shelving mounted to the wall over the long side of the L-shaped desk. A matching computer desk was positioned behind her chair and in front of a large window that overlooked the parking lot across the street, showcasing the view of the adjacent park where employees from the Cleveland Justice Center usually ate their lunch. Lately, you could see a constant presence of protesters from the Black Lives Matter movement mulling around the area.

As soon as Lisa hung up the phone, Richard announced, "Well, we have to find somebody quick. I'm getting behind in processing evidence for my detectives. And my office has been swamped with requests for reports, evidence and correspondence since the onset of the Tamir Rice case. The Justice Department is all over us, and the chief of police and mayor want every 'i' dotted and every 't' crossed. I need help!"

"I know that's right. How's Janice?" Richard felt her question totally dismissed the urgency of his situation.

After noticing how Afrocentric Lisa's office looked, Richard wondered how she felt about the Tamir Rice case. Did she hate the people she was responsible for hiring and firing? "She's good. Henry?" He returned her interest in spousal well-being.

"He's good. You, Janice and the kids going to the annual Memorial Day picnic this year?"

"We'll be there."

"What about James? Is he bringing his flavor of the week?"

"You know my brother will be there, and of course, with his flavor of the week. I don't think he ever dates any woman more than once—not since Pam."

"If I didn't know better, I'd say you sound a little jealous."

"Come on, Lisa. You know I'm happily married."

"Every man gets a little restless sometimes. How long have you and Janice been married now anyway?"

"Almost twenty years, I guess."

"You guess?" Lisa swirled around in her chair to pull out some files from the file drawer in her computer desk. "I hope Janice never hears you say that."

"She knows I love her. That's all that matters."

"I guess that is all that matters. I mean you had your chance like your brother James to sow your wild oats, right?" Lisa pulled her heavy set of extension braids behind her ears and bit her lip as if she were thinking about something.

"No. I'm nothing like James. Janice is my soulmate—my one and only lover!" The words had been more of a struggle to release than they had ever been before.

"Impressive. They don't make guys like you anymore." Lisa finally conceded. "You're the real McCoy!"

"Now, that's a saying I haven't heard in a long while. Be careful, you're telling your age." Richard stood to leave. "Well, I'll let you get back to your *interview*," he said with air quotes. The truth be told, Richard wanted to get away from Lisa because he felt like she could see right through him, and he didn't want her to discern the sense of restlessness that he'd been feeling. He hated the way he'd been looking at other women lately. He wanted to be the man that all the women he knew had admired for so many years—dependable, hard-working, trustworthy, loyal, faithful Lieutenant Richard Kemper.

"Yes, let me get back to it. I'll ask around to see if anyone knows of someone who may be interested and qualified for the position. I'll keep you posted. You better start asking around, too."

"I will. I'll check back with you by the end of the week," Richard agreed as he left the room, shaking his head about the female applicant as he passed her on his way back to his office.

7

Richard was so glad to get out of his office for some lunch and some man talk with his brother that he could have done a 'hallelujah' dance as he entered the Reasons Sports Bar and Grille across the street from the Justice Center on West 3rd. He took a seat at a booth and immediately noticed the server coming toward him. She looked to be in her twenties. He loved her smooth, caramel, silky skin. She wore a white button down blouse and black form fitting pants. Her figure was well-proportioned like a Coke bottle.

Here I go again! Richard scolded himself. He just didn't understand why he was noticing women so much lately. He decided it was a good thing that Janice couldn't read his mind.

"What can I get for you, Sir?" the server greeted him.

"I'll have a Coke, unfortunately," he told her. "I'm still on duty."

The server smiled, "My name is Janice by the way, and I'll be your server."

"Beautiful name," Richard added with a smile, "I'd like a glass of water, too before I order. I'm waiting on my brother."

Richard didn't want to think about all the work he had to get done before the day ended, so he began to immerse himself in the sounds of the restaurant. Though it was slightly crowded, the noise level seemed to be a low, murmur—men chatting, sports commentators discussing the NBA playoffs. It was an exciting time—the Cleveland Cavaliers had made it to the NBA Finals. The city wanted to be happy, but the agony and despair of the people, who wanted justice for Tamir Rice and others that had been gunned down by police officers in the previous months kept the mood of the city in a weird balance.

Nevertheless, the sports memorabilia that adorned the walls of the bar and grille along with the happy banter of the guests helped keep Richard's mind off of his need for a secretary for a few minutes here and there.

"What's up, Rich?" James, Richard's younger brother, said as he took a seat across from him in the booth. He was dressed in a navy police uniform with a build somewhat similar to Richard's. They both had dark, wavy hair, broad shoulders, an appropriate waist size and firm muscular arms and legs. Only their complexions differed a bit by a couple of shades, Richard being the darker one.

Richard extended his hand to shake his brother's. "Hey, Man. What's going on?" he responded.

"Trying to find a date for this Memorial Day picnic coming up," James said as he picked up the menu.

"Are you kidding me? You always have two or three women on standby."

"I know, but I'm tired of dating these hood rats. I'm ready for a real woman."

"Is that right?" Richard leaned back in his seat and surveyed his brother cautiously. He stared into his eyes for a few moments, searching for any detection of a lie.

"Yeah, you know anybody?" James stared back, daring him to find any deception.

"If I did, I wouldn't steer her toward you for you to break her heart and blame me."

"Man, I'm telling you. I think I just might be ready to settle down."

"Well, let's just say, I'll believe that when I see it. Hey, you know anybody I might be able to get to fill the secretarial position in my office." He stopped searching his brother's eyes, fully aware that James was the type of liar that even a lie detector machine couldn't catch.

"You find me a woman. I'll find you a secretary."

"Man, Be serious. You know with all this stuff going on with Internal Affairs and the Justice Department investigating all these police officers, I can't afford to be understaffed. Help a brother out!"

"I'll ask Sheila in Dispatch. I think I heard her mention she was trying to find a secretarial position for a friend of hers a few months ago."

The server returned and placed Richard's Coke on the table in front of him along with his water. "You gentlemen ready to order?" Her smile was warm, inviting and pleasant.

"That ain't all I'm ready for," James said as he looked the server over like evidence in a crime scene. She smiled and clicked her pen, holding her notepad up to indicate she was ready.

"I'll have a cheeseburger, fries and another Coke," Richard announced. He wanted to stare at the cleavage that peeked from her white blouse, but he knew better.

"I'll have the same, Young Lady—unless you're on the menu." James licked his lips and waited for a reply.

James annoyed Richard when he flirted sometimes, and Richard wasn't always sure if it was because he thought it was classless and immature or if he was jealous because he couldn't do it. He was glad when the server ignored James' flirting and remained professional.

"No, I'm not on the menu, Sir." She blushed slightly. "Would you like a Coke, too?"

"Yes, I would, Baby. And, what's with all the formalities? I'm James, and you are?"

"Janice." Her voice was timid.

"Now look at that, Rich. A Janice for you, and one for me. What you doing for dinner tonight, Baby?"

"I have to go put in these orders." The server almost tripped over her own feet, blushing and scrambling to get away from James.

"Did I say something wrong?" James asked with a sly grin. "Or maybe this policeman's uniform scared her."

Richard shook his head. "Ready to settle down, huh?" His eyes followed the young lady's behind until it was out of sight.

"Old habits die hard, my brother. You know that. But, it looks to me like, some habits are being resurrected!"

Richard looked away nervously. "What are you talking about?"

"You were checking her out harder than me," James declared.

"I was just trying to see what had you so interested." Richard took a sip of his Coke. "Just have Sheila get in touch with me if she has any leads on a secretary."

"I got you. But, we're gonna discuss this new roving eye of yours sometime soon."

8

Finally, the day ended, and Richard prepared to go home. He headed to the parking lot across the street from the Justice Center. It was empty. After all, it was after 5 pm. Mostly, everyone who worked first shift got off at 4:30, and they wasted no time leaving once the work day was over. Richard knew he needed to work even later than a half hour seeing that he had to do the work of his secretary.

Nevertheless, he felt much too anxious to focus on work. Maybe, he thought, he would go in early the next day and get a jump on things. It was still daylight, and the sun shone brightly. It gave him some optimism about finding a new secretary, as well as looking forward to enjoying the company of his wife and three sons when he got home. Lately, he'd been so distracted with work that he was irritable all the time when he came home.

He had almost made it to his car when he saw the woman from Dispatch that he and his brother had talked about during lunch, Sheila Willis. The lavender of the polo T-shirt she wore had a calming effect on him. He knew that Sheila was someone who he could trust to help him with his problem. She was a friend of James', and he had just said at lunch that she might know of someone who could fill his secretarial position.

"Hey, Sheila!" he called out to her.

She looked up. Even she looked good to him today, full-figured, voluptuous, a smile that could melt any man's heart—so genuine, so full of love. He admired the tight fit of her black jeans. She reminded him of the singer, Jill Scott.

"Hey, Lieutenant Kemper. How are you?" she said in a sweet tone as she approached.

"I'm good. I need to talk with you for a moment."

"Sure, what can I do for you?"

"I need a secretary. You know anyone?"

"I sure do. I have a friend who lives in Columbus. She's looking to relocate to Cleveland. I've been trying to find her a position here since February."

"That's great. What does she do in Columbus?"

"She's a legal secretary. She works for Attorney Belinda T. Caldwell."

"I've heard of her. She has a reputation for winning criminal cases—for the defendant. I'm glad we don't have anyone that strong with criminal cases here in Cleveland. She must be pretty good if she works for her. How can I get in touch with her?"

"I'll text you her number."

"I'd prefer if you forward her information to Lisa Brown in HR. I don't want to meet her until she gets past Lisa. Lisa knows what I need."

"No problem. I'll give her the information first thing in the morning. So, are you ready for the Memorial Day picnic?" Sheila asked him. She was walking a little bit ahead of Richard, and he admired her behind as she moved.

"Oh, you must be ready to lose in The Battle of the Sexes volleyball game this year?"

"Now, you know the men haven't beaten us in five years." She turned a little toward him now, and he took in her double-D breasts with an audible gasp. She didn't seem to notice.

He breathed a sigh of relief and said, "That's because volleyball is a ladies' game. Let's see what you can do on the basketball court."

"They don't have basketball courts at Big Creek."

He imagined her breasts jiggling as she ran up and down a basketball court wearing a jersey. "Lucky for you women! Come on. I'll walk you to your car."

"How's Janice?"

He felt a pang of guilt for what he'd been thinking. "She's great," he answered, noticing a female attorney from the prosecutor's office that he'd testified for in the past. He liked the way the calves of her legs looked as she walked with assured steps in red pumps. He followed her legs up to her red two-piece suit and her black blouse that covered two handfuls of perky breasts. He admired how kissable her lips always looked—glossed in moist red, and he glanced at them. Then, he checked to make sure that Sheila didn't notice him.

"Thanks for walking me to my car," she said.

"You're welcome. Don't forget to give that information to Lisa." He opened the car door for Sheila after he heard her click the remote to unlock the door of her gold 2012 Ford Focus. Full-figured woman like her should be driving a sedan, he thought. He caught a whiff of her fragrance. It smelled of wildflowers, and he wondered for a moment what it would be like to get wild with her. He smiled involuntarily.

"I won't." She positioned herself behind the wheel. He smiled again as he noticed how her large breasts nearly touched the steering wheel. He closed the door for her and forced himself to stop staring.

Sheila rolled down the window as she started her engine. "See you later," she told him as she put the car in reverse and began to pull out of her parking spot.

"Bye," he answered, turning his attention back to the attorney, but she had disappeared. His heart sank a little as he walked over to his black 2014 Chevy Impala.

9

Richard entered his kitchen through the deck entrance and was met with the smell of pork chops broiling in the oven. As he passed the stove, he could see though the clear lids of the pots that his wife was cooking green beans and white potatoes—no doubt with smoked turkey tails. His wife was a great cook.

He tried to get to his home office before she returned to the kitchen so as to have a few minutes alone before he had to engage in small talk with her. He wasn't in the mood for it, but he wasn't able to accomplish his goal.

"Hey, Rich. How was your day?" she said as she tried to embrace him for a hello kiss.

He sidestepped her and continued to his office, "It was okay. Give me a few minutes, okay? I have a few things I need to attend to before I'm ready for dinner." He gave her a peck on the cheek as he headed for his destination.

She looked hurt, but conceded to his request. "Sure. Dinner will be ready in about a half hour."

"Good. That's all the time I need. Where are the boys?" He called from his office, while she stayed in the kitchen.

"Tony is at band practice. Sonny is at baseball practice, and Junior went over AJ's house to play video games. I thought you were going to pick up Tony before you came home."

"Was I supposed to do that?" Richard yelled. He sat down on the sofa and took off his shoes so he could lay down for a bit.

"Yes, Rich. You were supposed to do that."

He hated her sarcasm sometimes. "Well, I'm home now. Text him and tell him to take the bus." He laid back and closed his eyes. He hoped that

Janice would fix the problem with Tony. No way was he going to pick him up after he'd already made it home. He didn't understand why he was saddled with the job of picking Tony up all the time anyway. Janice had been home most of the day. She took off for a doctor's appointment that morning. Would it have hurt her to go get Tony? So what if Tony's school, the Cleveland School of the Arts, was on the way home from his job. He was tired. For a few moments, he envied his brother James. James didn't have a wife or kids. He only had to be responsible for himself. He didn't have to come home to the same woman every night either. Why was he complaining to himself? He loved Janice. He just didn't understand why he was beginning to feel so restless lately.

He thought about the attorney with the red pumps. He imagined those beautiful thighs and calves flowing into those red pumps raised high in the air forming a V-shape around his waist or better yet, his neck. When his eyes journeyed from her hips to her breasts and then her face, it was no longer the attorney he saw, but his wife's stern glare, accusing him of infidelity. He shook his head to get rid of the image, but it seemed like the effort made his head hurt. He grabbed his head to try to give himself some relief, but it pounded as if someone were beating him.

Before he knew it, his half hour was up, and his wife was calling him to join her in the kitchen for dinner.

"Everything smells so good," he told her as he kissed her cheek again and admired the beautifully set glass dinette table. One candle in the middle, surrounded with a plate of broiled pork chops, a bowl full of green beans and white potatoes, a basket of perfectly browned dinner rolls topped with melted butter, a pitcher of lemonade, and two dinner plates with silverware for two. Her favorite song, Rock Me Tonight by Freddie Jackson played softly in the background.

"Thank you." She smiled as he pulled her chair out for her.

"The boys aren't coming home for dinner?" he asked as he stabbed two pork chops successively and placed them on his plate.

"Tony is going to practice with his group. Your brother picked up Sonny and is taking him to his house for dinner. He said he'd bring him home later, and Junior is still at his friend's house. He asked if he could stay there for dinner."

"So, it's just me and you?" Richard cut into his pork chop and put a piece into his mouth. He smiled at the taste.

"Good?" Janice asked as if her life depended on his response.

It annoyed him that after all these years, she still worried about whether he liked her cooking. He could feel the tension in the air as she anxiously awaited his critique. "Delicious," he answered, refusing to give her too much praise as he felt that she was fishing for a rapid succession of compliments like gunfire about how wonderful the meal tasted.

She exhaled. "How was your day?"

"Stressful. Still haven't found a secretary yet."

"You will."

"I know. It's just that losing Anna to the Chicago Police Department couldn't have come at a worse time."

"I can imagine. But, things are pretty bad in Chicago, too—maybe she wanted to be where she could make more of an impact on this whole police vs. Black people situation."

"You know, people just don't know what being caught in the middle is like unless they're Black and work for the police department." Richard grabbed his head.

"You still having headaches? You've been experiencing these headaches for almost a month now—ever since that perp you say you were wrestling with on that case banged your head on the concrete that night. What if you got a concussion or something? I don't know why you didn't get yourself checked out. You better make an appointment to see a doctor." Janice got up from her seat and began to rub his temples.

"Yeah. You got anything for me to take?"

"They're some extra strength Advil in the medicine cabinet in our bathroom upstairs. After dinner, why don't you go upstairs, take a couple and get in the shower. I'll come up and give you a relaxing massage when you're done."

"That sounds great, Baby. I think I'll take you up on that."

They finished dinner over small talk about their boys and their activities for the week. Janice agreed that she would do the car-pooling detail until Richard had time to see a doctor about his headaches and find a secretary for his office.

Feeling relieved about their new household responsibility agreement, Richard headed for the shower and thought that maybe if the Advil worked, he might enjoy making love to his wife tonight.

He went to the bathroom, took the Advil, and got in the shower. He still caught himself several times thinking about the attorney in the parking lot, the server at the restaurant, Lisa and Sheila—every woman but his wife, it appeared. He dried himself off after the shower and began to feel like the Advil might be working. When he came out of the bathroom and stepped into the master bedroom, Janice was standing in front of the bedroom window. She had on a yellow nightie that contrasted with her dark skin in a way that reminded him of a bumble bee instead of the attractive woman he knew his wife to be. Next, images of the Pittsburgh Steelers flashed through his mind. How he hated them as an avid Browns' fan. He felt a little nauseous.

"You ready for me?" she asked him.

He wanted to run back into the bathroom and throw up, but instead, he nodded in the affirmative and joined her at the window. They kissed, and he felt her hand on his behind. His body started to respond to her because her hands were warm and soft. He began to kiss her with more passion and intensity. The nauseous feeling subsided. She reached for a bottle of baby oil that was on the nightstand near their bed.

"Don't forget. I have something special for you," she told him.

He got on the bed and laid on his stomach. Janice straddled him and began to spread the baby oil on his back, moving her hands in a slow rhythmic motion down his thighs to his feet. Then, she massaged his temples. Next, she began to kiss his back, his neck, and he turned over. He was more than ready to be inside of her. She smiled down at him, and he thought she looked like the most beautiful angel he'd ever seen.

"I knew I loved my wife," he thought as she pushed herself down on him and took him all inside of her and began to move slowly.

"You're so big!" she praised him.

"You're so tight," he whispered.

He closed his eyes and began to enjoy the pleasure his wife was giving him when he heard a knock at their bedroom door.

"Mom. I'm home," Sonny's voice whined. "I need some help with my homework."

"Okay, Baby. Give mommy a minute," she said as she started to raise herself.

"No! Don't you dare leave me like this," Richard shouted in a loud whisper.

"I have to go, Rich." She pulled up some more.

"Please, Janice. Just finish."

"Rich, you know that you're going to take at least a half hour."

"I promise. I'll come quick."

She pulled all the way up, and Richard almost cried in anguish. "Janice!"

"We can continue this after I deal with the kids."

Richard turned over and prepared to pleasure himself as soon as she left the room. He knew that he wouldn't need her by the time she returned. He stroked himself and thought about the attorney with the red pumps.

10

A week later on a Monday morning at around 8:30 during the second week of May, Richard was at his desk at work, waiting to meet the woman that Sheila Willis said would make a great secretary for him. He hoped that she would live up to the legacy of his last secretary, Anna Wright. Anna was his 'work' wife. She knew what he needed before he even articulated it, and she ran his office with high efficiency. His phone rang, and he answered it immediately.

"Hello, this is Lieutenant Kemper's office."

"Pretty soon, you'll have someone else to say that," Lisa's voice was soothing, and her words were intoxicating. Richard wanted a secretary so bad, it felt like he was going through heroine withdrawal. "Where's Tamika? Why didn't she answer the phone?"

"You know Tamika. She's probably on a coffee break. Tamika was the receptionist for the detective unit. "When will the new applicant be here?"

"I'll send her up as soon as she completes the paperwork."

"How long do you think it will take to complete her training?"

"A couple of weeks, but I can do half day training so she can start helping you out as soon as possible."

"That's great, Lisa." Richard said, looking up to notice one of his detectives standing in his door, waiting for him to finish the call. He motioned for him to come in and take a seat. "I look forward to meeting her."

"Now, if you don't like her, let me know. I have a couple of others that I can let you interview, but they don't have her experience."

"I will. I gotta go."

"Alright. I'll talk to you soon."

"Detective Henderson, what can I do for you?" Richard asked after he hung up the phone. Like him, Henderson was in his mid-thirties and had worked in his department for about five years.

"Good morning, Lieutenant. I need to look over the forensics report for that East 30th Street case."

"Sure. I'll have it for you this afternoon." Richard got up and walked out into the adjoining office—his secretary's office and pulled a form from a row of shelves mounted to the wall near the desk. He returned to his office and handed the form to his detective. "Make sure you fill this out for me before you leave."

"You're handling these secretarial duties very well." The detective teased his boss as he began to complete the form.

"You don't want to joke with me about this, Henderson." He picked up the phone, dialed an extension, and said after a few seconds, "Yeah, I'm gonna need the forensics report on the Jeffrey Murphy murder investigation." He hung up the phone.

"Any word as to when you're getting a replacement?"

"I'm interviewing an applicant today."

"Why didn't you get a temp?"

"I can't have no temps in here with all the privileged information this office handles, especially with all the media attention this office has been getting lately. Everyone already thinks we're manipulating evidence to save one another from prosecution whenever there's an investigation into police conduct. Besides, Tamika helps me out with some of the clerical duties, but I'm afraid to trust her with anything really important." He gathered a few papers that were scattered across his desk together, and placed them in a silver 'to-do' tray on the edge of his cherry oak desk.

"I see your point. So, am I on your team this year for The Battle of the Sexes volleyball game at the annual Memorial Day picnic?"

"I don't know. Have you learned how to serve yet?" Richard laughed and retrieved a yellow legal pad from a desk drawer with a pen and began to scribble some notes.

"I know you ain't talking about the way I serve, Mr. Can't Even Get a Serve Over the Net."

"Who can't get a serve over the net? I know you ain't talking about me. Man, the last time I hit a serve to those weak ass women, they were bumping all into each other trying to hit it back, and they all missed it."

"And then, you woke up!" Detective Bobbie Johnson snapped as she entered the office. She was also in her mid-thirties, but she had only been with the department for the past two years.

"Oh, here we go!" Richard leaned back in his seat, grinning. "Man, we can't talk about the game no more. You know how sensitive the women get when they hear the truth about how they ain't 'got' no game!"

"Who ain't got no game? Let's see. Maybe it's the team who hasn't won a game in five years!"

"Johnson, why are you in my office?"

"What's up, Partner?" Henderson greeted her.

"I came to turn in my report on that Ferguson investigation."

"File it for me."

"Don't you want to read it first?"

"You know I'll be so glad when I get my new secretary. I'm tired of doing double duty. Put the report on my desk, Johnson."

She placed the file on Richard's desk and turned to leave. Richard noticed that her black slacks fit very nicely around her curvaceous hips. He bit his lip in an effort to punish himself for looking.

As she left, Henderson asked, "You bringing the wife and kids to the picnic?"

"Of course. Why would you ask that?"

"No reason," Henderson replied. "Well, I'll be back after lunch to pick up that report. Work on your serve, Boss. I want to finally have some bragging rights over Johnson. She'll be a bitch to work with if they win again."

"Alright now, Henderson. Watch your mouth. I don't want no problems from HR."

"My bad, Boss. And in that case, you don't want to cause no problems with HR either if you get my drift." Henderson winked at Richard and left.

Richard shook his head, partly because he wanted to shake off Henderson's insinuation, but also because his head was starting to hurt again. His phone rang again. "Hello. This is Lieutenant Kemper."

"Hey, Bro!" James said. Richard could tell he was happy about something.

"James! Are we on for lunch today?"

"Naw, Man. I got something to do, but can I come up and talk with you about something?"

"Sure. I think I have a few minutes before I start this interview for the new secretary."

"Oh! Great. Sheila must have come through for you."

"We'll see. Come on up. I don't have a lot of time."

He got up to look out of the picture window located behind his chair. The city's skyline in the daytime was comforting to him for some reason. Looking at it made him feel powerful and in complete control—like he was on top of the world—or at the very least—in charge of the City of Cleveland.

Henderson made the second man now that had caught wind of the lustful nature that was growing inside of him. The first was his brother James. He couldn't deny it any longer. He was becoming dissatisfied with his wife. He thought about how she had refused to finish him when Sonny knocked on the door and interrupted their lovemaking. In that moment, he both loved and hated her. His head ached so bad, he wanted to scream.

11

It's him! Kim thought as she entered Lieutenant Kemper's office on the second Monday in May at about 9 am. Standing with his back to her, facing a window that overlooked the city's skyline was a man who looked just like the man from her recurring dream. She was so excited she wanted to scream out loud.

"Lieutenant Kemper?" she asked in a soft voice.

He turned and looked at her. Their eyes locked for more time than was professional.

"Yes. You must be Kim Nelson."

"Yes. I am. Nice to meet you, Sir." Kim extended her hand for a handshake. She could feel the moisture in her hands. She wanted to snatch her hand back and wipe it on her red skirt so that she could try the handshake again, *but that's just silly*, she thought.

"Have a seat, Ms. Nelson."

Kim sat down quickly and crossed her long shapely legs in a way that made her red skirt rise and reveal a peek at her thigh. He sat down in his chair across from her at his cherry oak desk. Kim loved his eyes immediately. She never saw the eyes of the man in her dreams, but his eyes were just as she had imagined—brown, probing, warm with long lashes.

"So, let's get right into this. Tell me about your experience as a secretary in the law enforcement field."

"Well, I've been working as a legal secretary in Columbus for about five years with a very prominent criminal defense attorney. Her name is Belinda T. Caldwell."

"I've heard of her. She's worked on some very high profile cases."

"Yes. I assisted with depositions, managing files on evidence for cases, and typing witness statements."

"Very similar to the work here." He got up from his chair and went over to his coffee maker. "Would you like to join me?" He held a coffee mug up toward her.

Kim breathed in the aroma of the coffee. It made her feel warm and cozy, but when she drank it, she usually got jittery. "No. Thank you," she answered, clasping her hands together. She wanted to keep her poise. She felt as though if she held her hands together, she could hold herself together. She felt totally unhinged by this man's presence.

"What are your short-term goals?" He filled his mug with coffee, stirred in cream and sugar, and returned to his seat.

"Well, since I'm planning to move here to Cleveland from Columbus, I would like to get acclimated to my new hometown, meet some new people, and become a great administrative assistant or secretary in an office with lots of challenging and important responsibilities." Kim watched as he took his seat again. She allowed the scent of his cologne to bathe her. She recognized it as Calvin Klein's Euphoria. Len wore it, too, but she wouldn't hold that against him.

His dark navy suit and red tie stated his power and authority in his position firmly. When he spoke again, asking, "Your long-term goals?"

Kim didn't know how to respond for a few moments. She just sat there staring at him until he smiled. His teeth were unbelievably straight and as white as a virgin's wedding dress.

"Get married. Have a couple of kids. Retire with an organization where I feel that I have made a great contribution to society," Kim finally told him. She hoped that her answer was sufficient.

"You're beautiful," she heard him say.

"Excuse me." Kim couldn't believe her ears. Did he just say that she was beautiful? She looked at his manicured hands. He was wearing a silver wedding band. She felt her heart sink.

"The way you express yourself," he said in an enthusiastic tone. "It's beautiful."

"Thank you. Does that mean I'm hired?"

"I will tell Ms. Brown that she can schedule you for training starting next Monday."

"Have you found a place in Cleveland yet?"

"Yes. I believe I have. Do you know Sheila Willis?"

"I do. Sheila is the one who recommended you."

"Right. She's my best friend, and she just helped me find a great apartment in Euclid near where she lives."

"That's great. So, when will you be moving?"

"This weekend—now that I have the job."

"Did you hire movers? Or you having friends move you?"

"Well, I have my brother, Sheila's husband, and I also hired a couple of movers."

"I thought you said you were moving into an apartment—not a house." he laughed.

"I just want to make sure I don't put too much strain on anyone's back." Kim laughed too. She wanted to pinch herself. Lieutenant Kemper had to be the finest man she ever met, and if he made love anything like what she experienced in that dream, she knew he was the man for her.

"So, you're gonna be here just in time to prepare for the annual Memorial Day picnic. Did Sheila tell you about it?"

"No. I don't think she mentioned it, but it sounds like fun. I love picnics."

"Well, make sure you plan to come. I would love to get a chance to know you in an informal setting. Here in the office, we will be quite busy, especially since my last secretary has been gone for almost two months. We have a lot of catching up to do."

"I wouldn't miss it. Who are you coming with?"

He held up his left hand to show his wedding band, "The old wife and kids," he proclaimed. He bit his lip, and Kim thought he was flirting with her.

"Oh," she said in a soft voice.

"Well, Ms. Nelson. I don't have any more questions for you. So, I need to get back to work. I will call Lisa and tell her my decision. You should go back to her office now and get her instructions on what you should do next." He stood to his feet and extended his right hand for another handshake.

Kim made sure she rubbed her hands on her skirt this time before she shook his hand, but she held on to it longer than was appropriate.

He pulled away and gave her a strange look that told her that he was not interested in her flirting.

"See you next week, Lieutenant Kemper." She hoped she hadn't made him change his mind about hiring her.

12

"I can't believe that both your husband and my brother couldn't help me move today," Kim told Sheila as she propped open the entry door at the Euclid Apartments on Euclid Avenue in the city of Euclid—a suburb of Cleveland, Ohio. It was Saturday morning.

"Well, you know Damon would have been here if he didn't get called in to work."

"I know," Kim conceded as she stepped into her new apartment. She looked around as she dropped a box marked 'KITCHEN' on the floor. This apartment was so much more spacious than her Columbus apartment. It was clean and freshly painted. The walls were gray with white trim. The carpet in the living and dining area was grey, and the texture was plush. The kitchen floor was a light colored hardwood that matched the cabinets and the blades on the ceiling fan. As she stood there for a few moments, taking it all in, the movers came in with her red leather sofa.

"Where do you want this, Ma'am?" one of them asked.

"Right there by the picture window," she directed them. The red sofa would contrast nicely with the gray walls and the white verticals that hung over the beautiful window.

"So, how'd your interview go on Monday?" Sheila interrupted her thoughts as she placed a box marked, 'LIVING ROOM' on the floor.

"Obviously, it went great or else I wouldn't be making this move yet, Girlfriend." They laughed. "Why didn't you tell me how fine my boss is?" Kim said after she was sure the movers had gone back out to the truck. She looked at her friend as she unpacked her living room accessories. Sheila wasn't much of a decorator. She knew her job was to remove the items from the boxes and give them to Kim. She was dressed in purple velour jogging pants and a white V-neck cotton blouse that accentuated her ample bosom and complimented her smooth, caramel skin.

"Because he's married. So, in my mind, he's not fine." She passed her a white bowl that Kim placed on the coffee table. Kim admired Sheila's warm smile and voluptuous figure. She waited for her to pass her the red balls that looked like artificial pomegranates to go inside the white bowl.

Kim opened the box that Sheila placed on the floor and started taking out white throw pillows. She lined them up on the L-shaped red leather sofa so that they created a V-shape inside the L. "Well, I think he's the one for me, Girl." She ignored her friend's judgmental comment.

"You couldn't possibly be serious." Sheila handed the last pillow to her, and they both headed back out to the truck for more boxes.

"Put the chair next to the sofa," Kim said to one of the movers. "And you can put that table right there," she directed the second mover as she followed Sheila outside. "Sheila, he's the man in my dreams." She caught up with her, and they both grabbed boxes.

"Kim, how can a married man be the man of your dreams? Aren't you tired of all of your relationships ending with a man telling you he's not leaving his wife or his woman for you? I'm starting to wonder if it's safe to leave my husband around you."

They both were silent for a moment as the movers walked past them, heading to the truck for more furniture. Kim noticed one of the movers gawking at her as she bent over to sit her box on the ground for a moment while she tied her white Nike tennis shoes. She knew that men usually noticed when she wore her red cutoff shorts and her V-neck white cotton shirt that clung to her frame like a fitted sheet.

She picked up her box, and ignored the mover's gaze. "Don't go there, Sheila. I didn't say that he's the man *of* my dreams. I said he's the man *in* my dreams." They stepped back inside the apartment and placed boxes for the kitchen on the kitchen floor.

"What's the difference?" Sheila seemed a bit frustrated as she started to take canned goods out of boxes and place them on the counter.

Kim wondered how her red, white and black accessories would go with the light-colored wood of the cabinets and the ceiling fan. She dismissed the thought and turned her attention back to Sheila. "The day I tried to commit suicide—that night I had a dream. Remember. I told you about it."

She decided that she liked the color of the wood, and it would complement her accessories beautifully.

"Okay." Sheila continued to take out food items, but she looked at Kim with expectancy.

"Well, the man that I dreamed about is Lieutenant Richard Kemper." Kim began putting canned goods in the kitchen cabinets that were mounted to the wall.

"You should always put canned goods in the base cabinets," Sheila corrected her. "I thought you said you didn't see his face." She began taking the canned goods from the wall cabinets to place them in the base cabinets.

"I didn't. But, I saw the office. I saw his body. It was him. I know it!" Kim placed her canister set on a shelf over the sink.

"Kim, he's married." Sheila moved them to the kitchen counter. "They might fall off of there," she pointed out.

"Well, maybe he's having problems with his wife." Kim opened the refrigerator and placed a bottle of wine inside.

"I don't know a man who's happier with his wife than Lieutenant Richard Kemper." She took a seat at the kitchen table to rest a bit as she watched Kim place a red vase in the center of the table.

"Well, he was flirting with me in the interview." Kim sat across from Sheila at the table and admired the way the vase complimented the décor for a few seconds.

"Kim, some men just flirt to get you to do what they want." She searched a grocery bag that sat on the floor and pulled out a frozen pizza. She held it up for Kim's approval.

"What do you mean by that?" Kim nodded, got up and turned on the oven. Then, she went through a box of cookware.

Sheila joined her, giving her pots and pans to put away in the base cabinets. "Well, especially in work situations, some men feel that if they flirt with you a little, you'll do a better job or do a little extra."

"He told me he wanted me to come to the annual Memorial Day picnic so that he could get to know me better."

Sheila handed Kim the pizza pan. "Kim, you're starting to worry me. I'm telling you that it's not a good idea to set your sights on him. I don't want you to get hurt again. Please, let it go. I'll set you up with someone nice."

Kim knew that Sheila was not going to understand her connection to Richard Kemper so she agreed to let it go. "Okay, Girl. Well, you better set me up with somebody soon." She took the pizza pan, opened the frozen pizza and placed its contents on the pan.

Sheila took the pan from Kim and placed it in the oven. "Did Dr. Stevens refer you to a new therapist here in Cleveland?"

"Yes. Her name is Dr. Nancy Ball. I have an appointment with her in a couple of hours. So, we better get this stuff moved in quickly." She filled a bucket with ice and retrieved two wine glasses from the wall cabinets.

"Good. I'm glad to hear it. You want to go to church with me tomorrow?"

"Are you planning to hook me up with a deacon or something?"

"I don't think that any of the deacons at my church are ready for you!" She laughed as she opened another box. "Besides, all the deacons are married."

"Sheila, I hope you didn't bring me to this God-forsaken town just so that I can deal with the same lack of men I had to deal with in Columbus." She removed the wine from the refrigerator, opened it and poured it into the glasses. Then, she dropped two ice cubes in each glass.

"There are plenty of single men on the police force. I can introduce you to one of them every week," Sheila bragged. "I just want you to come to church because I think you need a little work on your moral compass." They clinked glasses and took a sip of the wine, smiling at each other— acknowledging their delight at being back together in the same city again.

"Well, I'm all for meeting these police officers, but I don't know about this moral compass!" Kim opened another box marked 'KITCHEN', and pulled out her wine rack.

13

Kim wanted to look nice when she had her first therapy session with Dr. Ball, so she showered and changed into a navy two piece jacket and skirt with a cream shell. She appreciated the fact that she didn't have to wait long when she let the receptionist know that she was there for her appointment. When she got to Dr. Ball's door, she stood at the entrance waiting for her.

"Good afternoon. You must be Kim Nelson," she said, welcoming her into the office and gesturing for her to take a seat on a black leather sofa located next to her light wood desk.

"Yes. That's me," Kim answered as she looked around at the office with a bit of apprehension.

The walls were yellow and the carpet was gray, but the chairs and the sofa were all black leather. Specks of purple from flowers, knick-knacks, and other accessories stood out against the yellow, gray and black of the room. A light wood bookcase sat in a corner by a window with white mini blinds. The smell of vanilla permeated the atmosphere and reminded Kim of when her mother baked sweet potato pies for the winter holidays. Kim assumed it was air freshener of some sort. A feeling of comfort, warmth and calmness overwhelmed her because of the cleanliness and organization of the office, the smell of violets mixed with vanilla and the comfort of the sofa. She noticed a bowl of peppermints on a small table next to the sofa where she was seated. The doctor pulled the chair that appeared to be meant for her guests up close to her.

"So, what brings you here?" she asked.

Kim was a bit annoyed by the question. Dr. Ball knew why she was there. After all, Dr. Stevens from Columbus had set it all up. She knew they had discussed her case, and Dr. Stevens had forwarded her file. Kim noticed

Dr. Ball's Bachelor of Science, Master of Psychology and Doctorate degrees lining the wall next to her desk. The Bachelor and Master degrees were from Cleveland State, but the Doctorate degree was from Case Western Reserve University. Her new therapist looked a bit motherly even though her attire was professional. She wore a black suit with a purple shell. She was more handsome than pretty with smooth dark skin, full lips and a stiff hairstyle that was cut short. Her frame was sturdy and unappealing.

"I tried to commit suicide," Kim answered in a matter-of-fact tone. She sat up straight and looked into Dr. Ball's eyes as if she were daring her to judge her.

"And how are you doing, now?" Dr. Ball leaned back into her chair, hit the record button on a small recorder, placed it on her desk and started to take notes on a yellow legal pad.

"I'm good." Kim repositioned herself on the sofa and leaned back, still staring at Dr. Ball with a firm glare.

"Dr. Stevens tells me that you're having some problems in your relationships with men."

"What relationships?" Kim said with a good deal of sarcasm in her tone.

"Ms. Nelson, you're going to have to cooperate if you want to get anything out of these sessions."

Kim crossed her legs and sighed. "I know. It's just that I'm feeling pretty good today. Like maybe there's no need for me to be here."

"Oh. Why is that?"

"I think I finally met 'the one,'" Kim admitted. She hoped that Dr. Ball would agree that therapy was unnecessary, and that, if she had indeed met 'the one,' it was time to celebrate and move on.

"Well, that's sound great. Who is he?"

Kim liked her enthusiasm. She felt encouraged. "My new boss. I start my new job on Monday, and my boss is a man that I dreamed about several months ago for the first time, and I keep having recurring dreams about him."

"Tell me about him."

Good! Kim thought. *She sounds positive, like she's on my side.* "He's handsome. He's powerful. He's attracted to me," Kim shared.

"Do you know if he's seeing someone?"

Kim thought she saw a frown on Dr. Ball's face, but she reasoned that she was just serious about her work. *Well, this would be the true test. How she responds to my answer to this question will tell if she really gets me.* "He's married," Kim stated, looking into Dr. Ball's eyes with urgent anticipation.

"Married?" She sat a little straighter in the chair, and she squirmed a bit as if she were uncomfortable.

"Yes. He's married, but I know he's not happy with his wife." Kim made the statement with the assurance of a newly converted Christian. Yet, the second attack on her faith came swift like a toddler who gets into trouble as soon as you turn your back.

"And how do you know that?" she asked.

Nevertheless, a true believer is always ready with an answer. "He flirted with me," Kim told her without as much as a blink of an eye or even a flinch.

"Ms. Nelson, I have to tell you that I don't think you should set your sights on a married man. After all, one of the reasons you admitted to attempting suicide is because you keep getting involved with men who are already committed to other women. Why start out with the same situation again?"

She sounds just like Sheila, Kim thought, but still, she stood ready to defend her faith. "I know that this time it will be different," Kim said with fierce determination.

"I have to strongly recommend that you keep your relationship with your boss a professional one."

"Well, you know what you can do with your recommendations!" Kim stood to her feet and stormed out of Dr. Ball's office. *I know in my heart that the man in my dreams is the man of my dreams, and I'm not going to let anyone turn me around!* Kim screamed in her mind. She resolved wholeheartedly to realize her dream no matter what anyone else thought.

14

The smell of Calvin Klein's Euphoria and coffee brewing made Kim feel as if she were on cloud nine. She was excited about her first day working with Lieutenant Kemper, the man *in* her dreams. Before speaking, she admired him as he stood in the picture window of his office looking out over the skyline again, giving her further confirmation that he was destined to be her man.

"Good morning, Mr. Kemper," I have your coffee. She placed the cup on his desk, and he turned to face her. She admired the fit of his gray suit that he wore with a yellow shirt and gray print necktie that showcased hints of yellow and royal blue. Although, she hated the fact the colors reminded her of Dr. Ball's office and her pronouncement that she should keep her relationship with her boss a professional one.

"Good morning, Ms. Nelson," he returned the greeting and sat down to his desk. He picked up the cup of coffee and took a sip. "Aahh! Black! Just what I needed today. I'm so tired. I needed something strong to keep me alert."

"Your cologne smells very nice."

"Thank you, Ms. Nelson. But, we have important work to do today. We don't have time for small talk. Are you ready?"

"I'm ready," she told him, holding up her pen and pad.

"Each morning, you need to look in your inbox and process the detectives' requests for reports. Then, you have to type their written reports and submit them to me for review. Next, you need to respond to all emails within 24 hours and answer my calls. If they are requests that you can handle, then, do so. If they are calls that I need to address personally, send them to my voice mail. I will let you know when I am expecting a call that you should put through to me immediately."

"Is there anything else?"

"Lastly, once I have reviewed a report from a detective, you will need to file it appropriately. Any questions?"

"No, Mr. Kemper. I'll get started right away."

"And remember, for the next two weeks, you will work here in the office in the mornings and then go to HR for training in the afternoons."

"I got it, Mr. Kemper." She noticed a picture of him with his family on his desk, and she picked it up. "Is this your wife?"

As he stood to his feet, he took the picture out of her hand, "Yes, it is, Ms. Nelson."

"Pretty."

"Thank you."

"Does she help you shop for your attire? That suits looks really good on you."

"Are you flirting with me, Ms. Nelson?"

"Is it that obvious?"

He blushed. "Ms. Nelson. Please don't do that. We have a lot of work to do." Suddenly, he grabbed his head.

"Mr. Kemper! Are you okay?" Kim ran to his side as he bent over, obviously in a lot of pain.

"It's just a headache," he grunted. "It'll pass. It always does."

"Have you seen a doctor?"

"I have an appointment in a couple of weeks."

"Well, is there anything I can do for you?" she asked, helping him to his chair.

"No. I'll be fine." He sat back in his chair, breathing heavily.

Kim started to massage his temples. "Does this help?"

He didn't answer right away. He seemed to be enjoying the massage. After a few moments, he responded, "Ms. Nelson, I'll be fine. Please get back to work. I just need some time alone."

Kim slowly released her fingers from his forehead, picked up her legal pad from his desk, and walked out of his office into her own, slowly.

She decided to go to the vending machine to get a snack. Eating always gave her comfort when she felt unhappy. And, making advances at her boss, who was obviously disinterested made her a little more than unhappy. As she neared the vending machine, a man in a police uniform approached and stood behind her.

"If you're hungry, why don't you let me take you to lunch in a couple of hours?" he asked, leaning in to whisper in her ear.

"Excuse me." Kim tried to sound annoyed.

"You heard me," he said, looking her over like one needs to look over a car in a police auction.

"I don't know you." Kim stated. She was somewhat intrigued by the police officer. He was handsome and reminded her a bit of her boss.

"Let me take you out," he reiterated.

Kim thought about the fact that she had another appointment with Dr. Ball the next day, and she wanted to be able to tell her that she had stopped pursuing her boss and was now interested in someone else so that she wouldn't have to hear her discourage her attraction to Mr. Kemper. Plus, she needed somebody to take her to that company picnic so that she could use it as an excuse to get close to Mr. Kemper when they were away from the job.

"Are you going to the Memorial Day picnic?" she asked.

"As a matter of fact I am," he told her as he took some change from his pocket and put it into the vending machine.

"I need a date. Would you like to go together?"

"I would." He took out his cell phone. "What's your choice?" he nodded toward the machine.

Kim told him the letter and number for a Snickers' bar.

He pushed the buttons, retrieved the candy, placed it in Kim's hand and asked, "Now, what's your number?"

Kim entered her number into his phone as he watched in anticipation and joy.

"Shame I have to wait all that time just to get a date with you," he complained.

"I'll be worth the wait."

"I bet you will," he agreed. He smiled as he watched Kim walk away, ripping the wrapper from the candy bar and taking a seductive bite.

15

Kim tried to ignore the pale yellow on the walls of Dr. Ball's office as she took her seat on the black leather sofa as she had done a few days ago on Saturday. She had agreed to see Dr. Ball on Saturday afternoons and Wednesday evenings after work. As she found herself constantly drawn to the color of the walls, she reasoned that yellow was supposed to cheer her up, but instead, it gave her a sick feeling, and the gray made her feel sad—even though the colors looked nice together, especially when she remembered how they had looked on Lieutenant Richard Kemper last Friday and how drawn to him the colors made her feel, but they just didn't have that effect in this office. In fact, it was just the opposite; she found the colors repulsive. Maybe, she felt, it had more to do with how she felt about Dr. Ball. She didn't like Dr. Ball because, like Sheila, this woman just couldn't see that Lieutenant Kemper was the man she'd longed for her whole life. She just didn't understand what that dream meant to her. The only thing that gave her comfort was the smell of the vanilla air freshener, which was always a constant presence.

"Good morning, Ms. Nelson. How are you feeling today? I hope better than Saturday," she said, biting her lip as if she wanted to say more, but decided against it.

"I feel great, Dr. Ball," Kim lied as she crossed her khaki-covered legs and pulled down her form-fitting orange knit T-shirt that tended to rise a bit, revealing her mid-drift.

"I'm so glad to hear that. May I call you Kim?"

Kim didn't believe she was glad to hear it. Kim thought it would please her to hear that she was falling apart. "Sure," she replied, and she looked her up and down as Bernie Mac would say, 'like she was short.'

Dr. Ball dismissed Kim's obvious dismay with her and glanced at the owl statue positioned on the corner of her desk. "Okay, Kim. Now, since our last session ended so abruptly, I didn't get a chance to hear the details of this recurring dream. Can you tell me about it today?" She pressed play on her pocket-size recorder and sat poised with pen and pad as she had done before.

"Sure. It starts with me entering an office. When I enter, I see a man standing with his back to me. He is standing in front of a big picture window, looking at the city's skyline. I turn away from him, and he comes up behind me. He massages my breasts and kisses my neck. We make love, and when I ask him if he thinks someone will catch us. He says it's okay because we're getting married soon."

"And you recognize this office as being your current bosses office?"

"I do."

"And you had this dream before you met your boss or visited his office?"

"Yes."

"But, you never actually saw the face of the man in the office."

"No. But, I know it's my boss."

"Well, Kim. All dreams are not literal. As a matter of fact, most dreams aren't. They're symbolic. The dream could simply have been about your desire to find the man of your dreams once you moved to Cleveland. Isn't that one of the reasons you moved here?"

"Yes, but I know it's more than that. I can feel it. Besides, I'd never seen the office prior to getting the job there. I saw the office in the dream before I saw it in reality."

"I'll have to do some research on that. How about some tea?" Dr. Ball said, putting her pen and pad in the chair and getting up to head toward the counter where she kept her liquid refreshments.

Kim knew the purpose of the tea was to help her to relax, but she didn't want to relax. She wanted Dr. Ball to acknowledge that there was something to her dream. "No, thank you," she told her as she folded her arms in a show of protest.

"How did your first week on the job go?" Dr. Ball asked as she poured a cup of hot water for herself and then dipped a tea bag into it.

"Great. By the way, you'll be happy to know that I accepted a date with a police officer to go to the company picnic in a couple of weeks."

"Are you sure you're ready to start dating again?" She put a couple of teaspoons of sugar in the tea.

"What is it with you?" Kim raised her voice in frustration. "First, you don't want me to pursue my boss, and now, you don't even want me to accept a date from a single man!"

Dr. Ball raised the cup to her lips for a sip, then decided against it. She sat the cup down again, firmly. "Kim, you don't seem emotionally ready for a new relationship right now. I think you need to focus on your mental and emotional health."

"Dr. Ball, do you have a man?" Kim sat straight up and peered into her eyes as if her own eyes were lie detectors.

"Yes. I'm married." Dr. Ball glanced at her wedding band.

Kim couldn't tell if Dr. Ball was admiring the ring or looking at it with disdain. "So, you got a man in your bed every night, right?"

"Ms. Nelson, we will not discuss my personal life." She walked away from the counter, picked up her notepad and pen and resumed her seat, leaving her tea on the counter.

"Oh it's Ms. Nelson now! What happened to Kim? Huh? Huh, Nancy? I thought we were becoming friends." Kim leaned forward into Dr. Ball's space as if daring her to continue their verbal sparring.

"You will address me as Dr. Ball, and I can't help you if you refuse to take my advice." Her face seemed calm and unwilling to argue with Kim.

"Look Dr. Ball! I'm lonely. I need a man. Advice is just that—advice. There's no law that says I have to do everything you tell me."

Dr. Ball's face softened more. "You're right, Kim. I just want to help you, but it is your decision."

"You damn right it's my decision. Are we done here for today?" It infuriated Kim that Dr. Ball was able to maintain her composure when for some reason she wanted to fight. She wanted to fight for the man in her dreams that everyone was so certain was a man that should never be more to her than her boss.

"Perhaps, it would be best for us to stop here for today. I'll see you next week, right?"

"I'll be here." Kim got up from the sofa and left Dr. Ball's office once again in a huff, and it seemed she could feel Dr. Ball's cool, calm smile on her back as she exited her office.

16

Richard wondered why Kim hadn't brought him his coffee yet this morning. She was usually all over him, and he had to admit that even though he tried to discourage her flirting, he was very much attracted to her. She always wore a lot of red outfits, and even though they were business casual, she made them look so sexy. He was often mesmerized by her big, brown eyes, her full soft lips and the perfect shape of her nose, and she smelled so good. He heard her tell Tamika one day that the name of her fragrance was Obsession. What an appropriate fragrance for a woman like her, he thought. He believed he had two reasons for feeling this way. First, she seemed *obsessed* with him—the way she constantly flirted with him and tried to please him. Also, the way he found himself thinking about her all the time, he often felt that he was *obsessed* with her—even though, she'd only been his secretary for nine days.

It was Thursday, just two days before the annual Memorial Day picnic, and he looked forward to seeing Kim in something really sexy. She was sure to wear some shorts in order to be comfortable for the volleyball game. He wondered who she planned to bring with her to the picnic. She mentioned that she had a date. He felt guilty again. He had no business thinking about his new secretary in this way. His head started to pound again, and he went into his drawer and grabbed a couple of Advil pain relievers. He went over to his office bar, which had everything to drink except liquor and poured a glass of water to wash down the pills. He had an appointment to see his doctor on Tuesday, but the headaches were starting to get so bad, he didn't think he could wait that long. If they got much worse, he decided that he would go to urgent care or the emergency room.

He put his head down on the desk and began to reminisce about his wife.

"Janice, are you coming? We're gonna be late!" the seventeen year old Richard yelled from Janice's front yard on Nathaniel Avenue. He didn't understand why she was taking so long to come outside. It was a nice spring day in May of 1997, just a few weeks before he and Janice were to graduate from Collinwood High School.

Finally, she came out of the house. She wore a yellow and white sundress. Richard remembered thinking that she looked like a ray of sunshine. She glowed as she moved toward him, but her facial expression was grim.

"What's wrong, Baby?" he asked.

She just handed him her books and kept walking. He admired the way her ebony ponytail rested softly against the chocolate nape of her neck. As his eyes roved her curvaceous frame, he felt a little turned on at how her hips filled out the summer dress and swayed so gracefully even though she was walking faster than usual. She seemed to be in a funk of some sort.

"Did I do something?" He tried to break the silence again as he sped up his pace to catch up with her.

"I'll say you did something," she snapped, but never broke her stride.

"I'm not a mind reader, Janice."

"Hey!" he heard his brother James call from behind them. "Wait up!"

"Where's Johnny? Can't you walk with him? I need to talk to Janice alone," he hollered back at his brother, who was running to meet them.

Janice kept walking faster. He jogged to catch her, and he yanked her arm. "What's wrong with you?" he shouted just in time for James to reach them.

"Hey, Man. Why you grabbing on her like that?" James said, giving him a push.

"This is my woman. You mind your business." He pushed James back.

"It's okay, James. I'm fine." Janice intervened.

"Rich knows better than to get physical with you, Janice." James got in between the two of them. "Are you sure you're okay?"

"I'm pregnant!" Janice blurted out.

Richard and James froze. "I guess you two do need to talk," James said after a few moments of silence. Then, he ran ahead of them.

"We need to go somewhere to be alone," Richard told her after several moments of walking in silence.

"What about school?" Janice said with tears welling up in her eyes.

"Hey, this is important. We have to talk about this, and we have to talk about it now. If our parents find out that we skipped school, we'll deal with it. If we miss any important school work, we'll just have to make it up."

"Okay." Janice conceded. "Where are we going?"

"Let's go to the park," Richard suggested.

"Okay," Janice agreed. They turned back and headed toward Mandalay Avenue.

They walked in silence, but when they got to the park, Janice took a seat on one of the swings on the playground. Richard started the conversation. "You know I love you, right?"

"I know."

"So, let's get married."

"Married? Just because I'm pregnant? This isn't the 60s, Rich. You don't have to marry me because I'm pregnant."

"Do your parents know?"

"No."

"Have you seen a doctor?"

"No. I took a pregnancy test."

"Janice, I want to be with you. I don't want our child coming into the world, and you and me apart. Marry me."

"What about college?"

"I don't want to go to college. I want to take the policemen's civil service test. I want to be a cop. They make good money and get good health benefits. I'll be able to take care of you and the baby."

"What if you don't pass?"

"I'll pass. And if you want, you can still go to college. You can go to Tri-C or Cleveland State. There's lots of colleges to choose from here in Cleveland."

"Sounds like you have it all figured out."

"Well, when the condom broke, I knew I had better start thinking about the possibility." He smiled at Janice and stood in front of her so that she swung right into him, and he grabbed her, pulling her off the swing into his arms. "I'm sorry about this, but I would love to start a family with you. I'll always love you. I know that."

"What do you think our parents will say?"

"They will be disappointed, but they'll just have to get over it."

Janice smiled. "Okay, I'll marry you."

"That's my girl. Hey, since you're already pregnant, and my parents are both gone to work, why don't we go back to my house and have an early honeymoon."

"Rich!"

"Come on. You feel better now, don't you? Everything is going to be fine. We might as well get used to doing it because when we get married, we'll be doing it all the time anyway."

"You're so silly." Janice laughed. "I'm glad you were my first."

"What you mean your first? I better be your only!"

"You are! Come on. Let's go."

Richard stood still, holding Janice in his arms. "Wait. Before we leave, I want to remember this moment forever. The moment when you agreed to be my wife." He held her as tight as he could and closed his eyes just as tight to capture the memory.

"Hey, are you okay?"

He felt her soft hands on his face.

"I love you, Baby." He opened his eyes and found himself staring into the eyes of his secretary.

"Why Mr. Kemper this is so sudden!" She teased him.

He wiped saliva from his mouth and tried to focus. "I must have fallen asleep," he explained.

"Yes. You must have. Do you always declare your love to your secretaries when you're dreaming?" Kim continued to tease him.

"I was declaring my love to my wife," he stated, straightening his tie as he raised his head from his desk. As he stood to his feet, she was so close to him that his face brushed against her breasts.

"I see," Kim replied. She looked as if she didn't believe him. "Here are some reports that you need to review today, and I need you to sign off on this stack of requests for reports." She laid the paperwork on his desk, and left the office.

Richard felt himself rise a little as he watched her hips sway in the form-fitting red dress. I've got to stop looking at other women like that, he told himself. He closed his eyes again.

"I do," he heard himself tell the pastor of his parent's church on his wedding day.

"Get this baby out of me!" he heard Janice scream while she squeezed his hand, and their firstborn son came into the world. A boy that looked so much like his big brother Anthony that he knew he had to make him his namesake.

"I love my wife," he told himself as he began to sign the reports on his desk after taking a few more Advil pain relievers for the headache that never seemed to subside.

17

When Richard entered Bar Louie's in Legacy Village, he saw that his brothers Anthony and Johnny were already seated in the bar area at a booth.

"Hey, what's going on?" he greeted them.

"Hey, Man!" Anthony greeted him first. "You alright? You don't look too good."

"I'm fine. Just been having some headaches."

"Well, you better get that checked out, Man," his brother Johnny chimed in.

"Yeah, I got it under control." Richard assured them. "Where's James?"

"He'll be here in a minute," Anthony told him as he beckoned a server to come take their order.

"Is it still happy hour?" Richard asked.

"Yeah. It's just 6. I don't think happy hour is over until 7," Anthony responded. "What you drinking? I got the tab today."

"I just want a beer."

Johnny looked around anxiously for the server, "Me too."

Once the server arrived to take their orders, James joined them. "What's up, Fellas?" he said as he approached, dressed in his policeman's uniform.

"Man, why'd you wear that?" Johnny complained. "Now, everybody is going to be looking at us funny."

"Yeah, but we'll probably get a few drinks on the house. Businesses love us."

"Man, you're a Cleveland police officer, and we're in Lyndhurst. You ain't got no jurisdiction up in here."

"Johnny, just shut up and have a drink! I want a Martini. Who's paying?" James rattled off his comments in quick succession.

"I got it, Man," Anthony answered. "So, who you bringing to the picnic this year, James?" When he asked the question, all the brothers got quiet and turned to look at James like the people in that E.F. Hutton commercial from the 70s.

"Man, I met a fine woman the other day at work, and I think she's new in town. I asked her to go with me to the picnic, and she agreed right away!"

"Yeah, she must be new in town." Anthony teased. "Anybody that works at the Justice Center should know to leave you alone. You done hit every single woman that works in the building. Haven't you?"

"Just about. But, I haven't seen her before."

"Well, if you guys don't mind, I'd rather not talk about James' sexual exploits tonight," Richard interjected.

"Yeah, I know what we need to talk about is how you were checking out that server the other day when we went to lunch," James reminded him.

"James, don't go there. You know I only have eyes for Janice."

"That was her name. Wasn't it?" James laughed at how his brother walked into that trap.

"Janice Kemper is the only woman for me," he reiterated.

"Well, any Janice can be made a Kemper if you put a ring on it." James continued.

"Let it go, James!"

"Hey, Rich. Calm down. What are you getting so mad about? James is just kidding you like he always does." Anthony said, waving the server over now with much more urgency.

"Can I get you guys something?" she said as she approached.

"We'll all have whatever you got on tap and a dirty Martini for this one," Anthony said, pointing to James.

"Are the Cavs playing tonight?" Johnny asked, trying to lighten the mood.

"I wanna know what's going on with Rich," James stated.

"Me, too," Anthony said.

"Ain't nothing going on with me, except I keep having these headaches, and I've spent weeks without a secretary. Now, I finally got one, but I have to train her at a time when the whole police department is under fire with the community about this excessive use of force issue. And Janice, well, she ain't satisfying me no more." Richard blurted out the last statement before he had time to think about it.

"Ain't satisfying you no more!" James shouted. Richard thought it made him happy to hear it.

"She's been distracted. You know, with the kids, work—the usual stuff married people have to deal with."

Anthony put his hand on Richard's shoulder and patted it. "That's the point, Rich. It's the usual stuff that married people go through. Don't let it get to you. You've been in the game long enough to know that by now."

"Yeah, but men need to be satisfied," James insisted.

"You got that right," Richard mumbled under his breath.

"What you gonna do?" Johnny asked.

"He's gonna get through it," Anthony jumped in before Richard could say anything. "Listen, Rich. Don't sweat it. Before you know it, you and Janice will be screwing like rabbits."

"How do you know?" James said. He loved to challenge Anthony in matters of the heart.

"You know how I know. I'm married."

"You ain't got no kids, though!" James argued. "I bet she ain't giving him none because of the kids!"

Johnny wanted some of the argument, too. "Well, Rich. Does it have anything to do with the kids?"

Rich shook his head. He went into his pocket and pulled out his last two Advil pills and threw them to the back of his throat and swallowed. "Well, she was riding me one evening, and Sonny, the mama's boy, knocked on the door, talking about he needed help with his homework, and she just got up off my erection to go help him. Can you believe that?"

"Damn," Anthony said.

"That's cold," James and Johnny said in unison.

Then, James added, "She would have had to sleep in Sonny's room if she had pulled that mess on me."

"She at least owe you some head or something," Johnny said, laughing.

"Guys, this ain't no joking matter." Anthony tried to keep a straight face, but Richard knew he wanted to laugh with James and Johnny. "Like

I said, Rich. These things happen in marriage, you've been married for almost two decades. I'm sure you guys have had problems like this before."

"Sex has never been a problem for us. You guys know that sex is what led us to get married in the first place. Remember, your namesake, Ant."

"Man, I can't lie. I would have been mad as hell if my wife left me like that. What did you do? Get yourself off?" Anthony started to laugh in spite of himself.

"You think I didn't!" Richard looked around for the server. He really needed that beer if he was going to put up with his brothers teasing him.

"Well, did she at least make it up to you the next day?" Anthony asked.

"Hell no!"

"Maybe you guys need to talk," Anthony suggested.

James pounded his fist on the table, "You guys need to f---!"

"Here's your drinks, guys," the server interrupted before James could finish his statement.

Anthony took a long, loud swig of his beer. "Just hang in there, Rich. Things will get better."

"Or you can go back to Reasons and see if that server will straighten you out," James declared.

"Don't do that, Rich. Stay faithful to your wife. You guys love each other. James is the last person you should listen to. He's a committed bachelor."

"I don't know about that, Ant." James downed his Martini in one gulp. "That woman I met at work might be the one."

"Man, get out of here!" Richard waved his hand at him in disbelief.

"Wait until you guys meet her at the picnic," James bragged. "You'll see."

"We can't wait," they all said in unison.

18

It was just after 10 p.m. when Richard got home from hanging out with his brothers. The house was surprisingly quiet. The boys must all be at sleepovers or something, he thought. He went into the bedroom. Janice was in bed reading. He went into their walk-in closet, shed his clothes quickly, leaving on his gray boxer briefs. He saw that Janice had on her yellow silk gown. For some reason, she thought yellow was sexy. I guess because he used to tell her how good it looked against her chocolate complexion when they were falling in love as teens. She still looked good in it. It was just getting old. He wished she would wear some red sometimes, like Kim. She looked so sexy in that red skirt when she went swaying those curvaceous hips out of his office today.

"How was your day?" he heard Janice say.

He didn't really want to talk to her. So, he ignored the question as he slipped under the covers in the bed next to her. He picked up the remote control to the television.

"How's the new secretary working out?" She posed the new question as if she hadn't noticed that he was ignoring her.

"Where are the boys?" he asked, turning on the television.

"They're asleep. Do you know what time it is? They have school tomorrow," she told him as she turned a page in her book, giving Richard a look that said, *Really! You're going to turn on the television when you see I'm trying to read.* "They all have sleepovers tomorrow night, so we can sleep in on Saturday morning," she told him with an exasperated sigh. Then, she turned on her side with her back to him, and her butt brushed against his hand under the covers.

Immediately, he wanted an orgasm, and he didn't care if he didn't get any sleep all night or all day while he was working for it. Although he knew it would probably only take a few minutes, considering how much he needed it. However, he was so frustrated, it was as if he just didn't know how to seduce his wife anymore.

"I wish you would consult with me before you give the boys permission to sleep away from home. It's dangerous these days, and did you forget that we have the picnic on Saturday?" he fussed, which he knew was a mistake before the words came out of his mouth.

Janice looked over her shoulder at him, still holding tight to her novel. "We've been married for almost twenty years, and I have never had to consult with you about sleepovers before!" He could tell she was really hot as she continued her rant. "We know the families where they're staying very well, and you've even given them permission to stay at their friends' homes when I wasn't around. Why are you getting all sensitive about everything now?"

He didn't know how to broach the subject, so he just blurted out, "Why aren't you taking care of me, Janice?" He began to channel surf.

"Taking care of you?" Janice laid the book in her lap.

"I need some sex."

"I do, too. What else is new?"

"That's your response?" He sat up in the bed. She still had her back to him with her head in the book. He wanted to snatch it from her. "Yes. That's my response," she answered, not even looking up from the book.

"Can you take care of your husband?" he asked in an angry tone as he got out of bed and paced the floor.

"Are you insinuating that I'm not taking care you and our children, Rich?" She held the book close to her chest and looked up at him.

"Take that however you want to take it, Janice. But, you're on some bull! You need to satisfy me!"

"Ain't nobody 'bout to give you none with you asking like that! Who do you think you're talking to?" She returned her eyes back to her book. This time, he knew she was finished with the conversation.

He knew that he should have expressed himself to his wife with more tenderness, but his erection seemed to be the one really doing the talking, and it didn't seem to want to ask nicely.

"I'm about to go downstairs and watch some television," he shouted as he grabbed a pillow and a blanket. Instinctively, he knew that he and his hand were about to get very well acquainted in a few minutes.

"Good! Now, I can read my book in peace."

"That's what you really want to do, Janice? Read? Really?" He grabbed his crotch. "So, you don't want none of this?"

Janice laughed and grabbed her crotch through the yellow, gray and white comforter that covered her and the bed. "I can't tell you want none of this! Not talking to me like that!" She yelled back at him.

Richard stormed out of the room and slammed the door.

19

Richard was still upset with Janice when he came home the next day from work. He came in through the back door and peeped into the kitchen from the corridor that led to the basement. Janice was frying tilapia. He knew that this was her way of getting back at him for their fight, and for some reason, she believed it was some kind of law that people should eat fish on Friday.

He hated seafood, especially tilapia. I guess she expected him to get dinner for himself. He wished he hadn't even come home. He could have hung out with his brothers or some of his detective friends from work. Although it seemed that since he'd been promoted to Lieutenant five years earlier, the detectives had distanced themselves from him. He understood, though. They felt like things were different now. He was their supervisor instead of a co-worker.

He decided that he'd go down to his man cave to finish watching Shaft, the first one. That's what he had watched last night when he left Janice in the bedroom alone. He had fallen asleep in the middle of it, and he wanted to see that love scene. Watching Shaft reminded him that he was a strong, successful cop. He had solved lots of the homicides in Cleveland, and he was respected among his peers. Shaft always got the villain, and he looked cool doing it. Growing up watching old videotapes of Shaft movies with his father is what made him want to be a cop. Born in 1980, Richard wasn't able to experience Shaft in its heyday, but his father told him stories about how much pride the Shaft movies gave Black men in the 70s. Richard knew after watching the movies time and time again, he wanted the Black community to be proud of his police work—the problem was that Blacks were anything, but proud of Black cops nowadays. Most Blacks saw cops as their natural enemies.

Nevertheless, he nurtured his fantasy with Shaft movies, and right now, it wasn't the Black community that concerned him, but his desire to be satisfied sexually. He knew that he'd have to deal with Janice's lack of affection for at least a few days. So, he decided to order a pizza for dinner and be satisfied with spending a few hours alone, watching his hero and idol. He popped the top on a beer he'd gotten out of the refrigerator he kept in his man cave and plopped down onto his black leather sofa, picking up their cordless landline to call Pizza Hut. As he waited for someone to answer, he picked up the remote control to his 60' flat screen and turned it on along with the DVD player and hit play.

"Rich!" he heard Janice yell after he had placed his order and hung up the phone. He ignored her. He'd teach her for frying tilapia on him. He heard her stomping down the stairs, and he thought about pretending he was asleep.

He settled back into a more comfortable position on the sofa to relax and watch his movie. He wished he had stopped by Walgreen's and picked up some more Advil as his head started to pound with excruciating pain— pain almost impossible to ignore. He had used up his supply.

"Rich," Janice said as she approached.

He had closed his eyes moments before she hit the last stair step. He hesitated before he responded, "What is it, Janice?" he said in a cool tone.

"How come you didn't pick up Sonny?" she asked.

"Why didn't you?" His response was flippant. "Last night, you said they were all going on sleepovers."

"Rich, you told me this morning that you'd pick him up from his baseball practice and take him to his friend's house for the sleepover. I agreed to get Tony and Junior. Remember?"

Richard began to rub his temples, "I guess I forgot," he admitted.

"I'll ask Anthony to get him again. Sonny can go to the picnic with him tomorrow, and we can pick up Tony and Junior on the way in the morning." Janice resolved the dilemma as was her custom. Richard turned his attention back to the television.

As he watched the love scene, he thought about Kim, and how sexy she looked in that red skirt today. He immersed himself in the memory of her cleavage that emerged from her low cut white blouse. He imagined thrusting himself inside of her as hard as he could. He could hear her screaming, 'It's yours, Big Daddy!'

He wanted her so bad, he thought he would bust. He picked up the phone and called her as he unzipped his pants and began to massage himself.

"Hello." Her voice was melodic.

"Hi, uh, Kim?"

"Yes. Is that you, Lieutenant Kemper?"

He wondered what excuse he could give for calling her. "You still coming to the picnic, tomorrow?" he asked.

"Sure, Mr. Kemper."

"I wondered if you could go by the office on your way and pick up some papers for me."

"Anything for you, Mr. Kemper."

That comment really helped to arouse him more. "You spoil me, Kim. What are you doing home on a Friday evening?"

"I'm still organizing and unpacking—getting settled in my new apartment. Besides, I want the place to look nice in case my date wants to come in tomorrow before or after the picnic."

Richard wanted to continue making small talk to keep Kim on the phone. He needed to hear her voice while he stroked himself. He imagined her riding him as he closed his eyes and let her soft voice increase his erection. It amazed him how much she turned him on. "I bet you have a nice place. Where did you say you live?"

"The Euclid Apartments."

He strained to keep his voice sounding normal even though, he was getting close to his orgasm, "Those are nice." He almost moaned the words.

"Are you okay, Mr. Kemper?"

"Yeah," he whispered.

"You sound a little strange."

"I'm lifting weights," he lied.

"Well, Mr. Kemper, if you get in any better shape, you'll be fighting the women off."

"You're such a flirt. How many broken hearts did you leave back in Columbus?"

"I'm sorry to say, I only left one broken heart in Columbus, and it was mine."

"I can't imagine anyone would ever want to hurt you." He was getting so close, he thought he could barely contain himself.

"I can't imagine any wife neglecting a man like you."

"Aaaaah, my wife, aaaah doesn't neglect me," Richard managed to get the words out as he climaxed all over his hand. "What gave you that impression?"

"Mr. Kemper. I see the way you look at me. And, are you sure you can lift those weights and hold the telephone? Or do you have me on speaker?"

"Aaaaah, Kim. I think I better get off the phone." He pressed the end call button before she could say anything else. Then, he slipped into the bathroom to clean himself up.

20

Richard and Janice unloaded their van with the help of their boys, and began to set up a table in the pavilion at Big Creek Reservation in Parma, Ohio—a suburb of Cleveland's west side. The sun shone brightly, and the day promised adventure, fun and family unity. Though, Richard felt a bit better than he had after his fantasy with Kim, he still longed to have a woman's body close to him. The smell of fresh air and the warmth of the sun on his arms gave him hope that he'd be able to shake off his sexual desires and enjoy his boys, his co-workers and maybe even his wife.

"How'd you enjoy your Uncle Ant," Richard asked Sonny as they set up the net for the volleyball game.

"It was cool. We ordered pizza and watched the game. I didn't expect the Cavs to make it this far, but LeBron is back!"

"Yeah, we're looking good."

"Look, Dad. It's Uncle James, and look at that girl he brought with him. She's hot!"

"Watch your mouth, Young Man." Richard looked up, and he couldn't believe his eyes.

Kim Nelson, his secretary was walking toward him with his brother, James. And she had on the sexiest pair of red shorts he'd ever seen and a form-fitting low cut white blouse that revealed quite a bit of her cleavage. He felt himself getting aroused even more than he had the night before. He was grateful for the loose-fitting jogging shorts he wore.

"What's up, Bro?" James greeted him. Richard could tell he was as happy as he'd ever known him to be.

"Hey, James. What's up?" he said. He could hardly speak.

"Hi, Lieutenant Kemper," Kim said, smiling.

Kim's smile made him throb. "James, why didn't you tell me you were bringing my secretary?"

"I didn't know she was your secretary when we met."

"Where did you meet her?" He knelt down to pound the stake in the ground that held one end of the volleyball net into the ground. He glanced up at his brother, awaiting the answer to his question.

James stared at Kim as if he were mesmerized. "I met her at the vending machine at work."

"I didn't know you guys were brothers." Kim hit Richard on the arm, playfully as he stood to his feet.

Her touch aroused him even more. He backed away from her and frowned. Kim looked confused. "Are you okay?"

"Yeah, yeah." Richard stretch to relieve the pain in his knees from kneeling, and his head started to ache. He went to adjust the stake on the other side of the net. "It's just that I'm getting another headache."

"I'll be glad when you see the doctor about those headaches," Kim said, looking at him with concern.

James grabbed her hand, "Me, too. When you'd say your appointment is? Tuesday?"

"Yeah," Richard answered. His voice was almost a whisper.

"Well, if you're going to be okay. I want to introduce Kim to the family," James said, pulling Kim toward the shelter where Janice, Anthony and Richard's sons were still setting up their table with food, drink and games.

"Yeah, you guys go ahead. Sonny and me are going to finish setting up this net so that the men can beat the hell out the women in this volleyball game. Right, Sonny?"

"You got that right, Dad!" Sonny answered.

"Hey, maybe we can go hiking on the trail after the game?" Richard called after his brother and Kim as they walked away from him.

"Bet!" James responded.

Richard was almost too distracted by Kim to finish putting up the net. His headache was getting worse. He searched the pockets of his gray jogging suit for his Advil.

"Hey, Tony. Can you get me a bottle of water from the shelter?" he told his son.

Tony complied with no question and in less than two minutes, he was throwing a bottle of water at Richard for him to catch.

Richard threw back the Advil and took a swig of the water. "Hey, let's get this game started," he shouted to everyone at the pavilion.

He could see that most of the major players had arrived, and it was their custom for those who were part of the police department to play the Battle of the Sexes volleyball game while spouses and significant others prepared the food for lunch. After lunch, they would go for a hike on the trail, and come back for another bite to eat and their Karaoke talent show.

Richard found it difficult to play volleyball because of his headaches, but he struggled through the game and was ecstatic to lead the men to their first victory in five years over the women.

"James, you must have got some last night. I don't think I've ever seen you play that good!" Anthony told his brother.

"Man, I think it's more that I'm excited that I might get some tonight!" James said, looking at Kim who was at the pavilion helping Janice prepare their lunch.

"Man, you just met her!" Richard jumped in. It was obvious that the idea of James sleeping with Kim did not agree with him at all.

"You sound like you jealous, Bro!" James teased.

"Well, you know he ain't getting none," Johnny added as the brothers began to separate from the others and head to the pavilion.

"You right!" James laughed and gave his twin a high five.

"Don't do that," Anthony warned his brothers. "Y'all need to take it easy on Rich."

"It's cool," Richard conceded. "I don't need their sympathy. Janice and I will be back on track before you know it."

"That's right, Rich." Anthony smiled at him with a look of approval and pride.

"Man, y'all ready to go out on the trail?" James asked, sounding exasperated. Richard guessed that James hated whenever Anthony chastised them for teasing Richard.

He smiled in triumph. "Yeah. Let's go."

"We gotta eat first!" Johnny ran into the pavilion and grabbed a couple of hotdogs.

They all enjoyed hotdogs, burgers, chicken wings, chips, cookies, pop and water. They talked about the community climate with the impending decision about the Tamir Rice case. They talked about other cases that were in the news and how difficult it was to work with the community now that they were viewed as the enemy.

Finally, everyone had eaten and talked enough. Most knew that a good walk or hike on the trail was just what they needed after eating.

"Kim, you want to go for a hike with us?" James asked, grabbing her hand and looking into her eyes like he was a lovesick puppy.

"Sure," she told him.

Richard noticed that even though she was with his brother, she wasn't able to keep her eyes off him. It made him feel desired. Every time he looked at Janice, she was in a huddle with Sonny laughing and talking about something that was their little secret. It bothered him that his only athletic son had turned out to be a mama's boy. He expected his musician son, Tony, to be the mama's boy or even his video geek nerd namesake, Junior, but not his football, basketball, and track star!

Richard followed as a group of about seven or eight of the police department support staff, detectives and officers, including his brother James and his secretary, Kim started toward the trail. "Janice, you coming?" he asked as he walked away.

"No, me and the boys are gonna hang out here. We have some other games that we want to play," she answered.

He barely acknowledged her response as he followed the sway of Kim's hips into the trees and started the trail.

His detectives, Bobbie Johnson and Mike Henderson, were talking to him about some cases as they walked, but he wasn't paying attention to anything they were saying. He couldn't keep his eyes off James and Kim. They were holding hands, smiling, looking like they were enjoying each other's company. His headache seemed to intensify the more he noticed how happy they seemed in each other's company.

"Hey, Lieutenant!" Henderson called to him.

"Yeah," Richard answered.

"Where were you? I called your name about four times!" he said with frustration in his voice.

"Sorry, Man. What is it?"

"You wanna race with us? We're gonna see who can get back to the pavilion first."

"I don't really feel like running or jogging. My head hurts," Richard admitted.

Kim turned around and looked at Richard. The concern in her eyes melted his heart.

"Why don't you guys go ahead? I'll stay with my boss and see him back to the pavilion," she announced.

"Alright," James agreed. "We'll meet you guys back there."

The group started jogging away in different directions as Richard sat on a tree stump to rest for a few minutes.

"Are you okay?" Kim asked as she sat beside him.

"I'm good," he told her. "I don't know why I'm having these headaches." He held his head as if his life depended on it.

"Did you bump your head on anything?" Richard could see the concern in her eyes, and he wanted so much to embrace her.

"Come to think of it. I did bump my head on the concrete during a big arrest a couple of months ago."

"Why were *you* in the field?" she asked.

"I always go out in the field on a case of that magnitude." He put his whole face in his hands and rested his elbows on his knees.

"Well, you think maybe you should go to emergency?"

"I hate the long wait in the emergency room. I'm sure I'll be fine until Tuesday when I have my appointment with the doctor."

Kim put her hand on his thigh, "I hope you're right."

Richard felt aroused again. He couldn't believe how much he wanted Kim. He'd never even looked at another woman since he met Janice. But, all he seemed to be able to think about now was how she neglected him and how sexy Kim looked in her outfits. He loved her caramel complexion, the silkiness of her skin, the whiteness of her smile, the softness of her hair—or her weave. Then, the smell of that Obsession perfume—it was intoxicating.

He put his hand on top of hers. She looked at him. He looked at her, and before he realized what he was doing, he kissed her. It was as if her lips were a magnet and his were steel. He couldn't pull himself away. His lips seemed to melt into hers, and she slipped her tongue into his mouth and it reminded him of what he imagined it felt like to be inside of her when he was masturbating to her voice the previous night. He imagined she was warm, wet and soft inside—just like her tongue. He saw a flash of Janice on the night that they conceived Tony in the backseat of his father's car at the park. He remembered how much in love he was with her. He remembered how good she felt when he made love to her. He pulled his lips away from Kim's slowly.

"I'm sorry," he said.

"It's okay," Kim responded. She looked embarrassed. She stood to her feet. "We better get back unless…"

"Yeah. We better get back," Richard interrupted and agreed with her.

They walked back to the pavilion and before they reached the others, Richard said, "That kiss was a mistake. It can't happen again, and let's not ever discuss it or mention it."

"Fine," Kim said. She walked away from him and went to join James.

After the Karaoke talent show, everyone was more than ready to end the festivities and go home. When Richard, Janice and their boys started to load their van, his brothers and all the other employees of the police department had already loaded up and made their departure.

"So, you guys finally beat the women this year!" Janice commended Richard.

He smiled, and then, he felt the most excruciating pain in his head he had ever felt. In a flash, he hit the ground.

21

It was the first Monday in June about a week after the annual Memorial Day Picnic. Kim and Sheila walked from the Justice Center to the Galleria for lunch at McDonald's. As they entered, they dodged people rushing in and out of the food court, trying to get back to work before their lunch hours were over.

The smell of summer's approach was in the air, and Kim felt happier than she had in months. "I'll have a fish filet meal," she told the clerk after Sheila had ordered a Big Mac meal.

"So, what did you and James end up doing after the picnic?" Sheila asked after they found a seat at one of the small glass tables with white trim and white metal chairs.

"He took me back to my place, of course," Kim said, eating her fries three or four at a time. "That's a pretty green," she told Sheila, admiring the mint green jeans she wore with a white polo and the matching mint green logo. Kim loved the way Sheila wore her hair with so many long, flowing curls. It made her look thinner, she thought. Sheila was proud of her full-figured body, but Kim always thought she could stand to lose a few pounds.

"So, any chemistry?" Sheila started to eat her fries as well.

They both gorged the fries down their mouths, trying to rush so that they could finish everything in time to get back to work.

"The only chemistry I felt was for his brother," Kim admitted.

"Richard?" Sheila seemed upset with Kim's announcement. She started to eat her fries one at a time.

"I told you that he's the man in my dreams." Kim took a bite out of her fish sandwich, and sat back in her chair as if she wanted to savor either the thought of her boss or the taste of her sandwich for a while.

"Kim, I told you that he's married. You met his wife. You socialized with her at the picnic. Don't you have a conscious? You can't be serious about pursuing this man, especially after all you've been through!"

Kim took a swig of her Coke. "I can't help how I feel, Sheila."

"You can, and you will." The determination in her voice was strong, but Kim was not moved. Sheila rolled her eyes at a woman who turned and looked at her from a nearby table and gave her a look that said, '*Why don't you get you some business!*'

The woman looked back at her as if to say, '*I wouldn't be in your business if you weren't so damned loud!*'

"You don't understand, Sheila." She brushed the bang of her shoulder-length, jet black wrap from her eye, and looked down at her white form fitting business casual dress to see if she had wasted any of the tartar sauce that oozed from her fish sandwich on it.

"No, *you* don't understand! I can't stand by and let you get hurt again. Don't you know that Richard loves his wife? He will never leave her. They have three kids. Do you really want to break up their home by getting involved with him? Besides, he would never give you the time of day." Sheila grabbed her Coke firmly and rammed the straw in her mouth, taking hard sips. Her eyebrows furrowed, and Kim could tell that she was about to bust.

"Oh, he already gave me the time of day," Kim bragged. She smacked her fries hard, hoping her show of confidence and bravado would cause her best friend to back off.

"What are you talking about, Kim?" she asked as she attempted to pick up her Coke, but instead knocked it over, causing it to spill all over the table. Grabbing a stack of napkins to dab the wasted beverage, she kept her eyes firmly on Kim.

Kim waited about three beats before she answered—desiring to make her next statement as dramatic as possible. "Well, when we were at the picnic, he kissed me." She smiled with a show of triumph as she watched Sheila's eyes widen with amazement.

"He what?" Sheila shouted so loud that about six or seven people turned from eating their meals to stare at her.

"He kissed me," Kim announced again with pride. She puckered her lips and blew an air kiss at Sheila to taunt her.

"Have you told your therapist about this?" Sheila asked. If she were a cartoon, Kim could imagine smoke coming out of her ears because she was so angry. Kim watched quietly as she dumped the wads of wet napkins into her empty McDonald's bag.

"I don't have to tell her everything that happens in my life." Kim crumpled her red fry box and put it into her McDonald's bag. She took another bite of the sandwich, savoring it once again.

"Kim, have you forgotten that she is supposed to help you get involved in healthy romantic relationships? Remember, Len? Remember, I had to take you to the hospital because you tried to kill yourself! Remember, you were so depressed to discover that *he* was married?"

Kim looked to see if the woman at the nearby table was still listening to their conversation. *Now, Sheila was pushing it* she thought. She all but told the whole Galleria that she had attempted suicide. If she didn't quiet down, Kim thought she might have to check her. "This is different," she said in a hushed tone after a few moments of silence—hoping Sheila would get the hint to keep her voice down. "I *know* Richard is married. He isn't lying to me. As a matter of fact, he's doing the very opposite. He's not pursuing me. He's trying to be faithful to his wife, but he can't resist me, and I'm telling you that's a sign."

"A sign that you've lost your mind!" Sheila scoffed at Kim as she stuffed her fry box into a bag and hastily opened her Big Mac box, took off the top bun, and began to squirt ketchup over the top piece of meat that barely peeked from under cheese, lettuce and special sauce.

"No. A sign that we are destined to be together. He's the man in my dreams, and he is attracted to me. I know he is. He is getting close to being unfaithful to his wife. And, if I can get a loyal man like him to cheat on his wife, I can get him to leave his wife. And if I can get him to leave his wife, I can get him to make *me* his wife."

"I hope you know that there's a saying that goes how you get him is how he'll be lost!" She started to rummage her purse as if she were looking for something.

"Once I get him, he won't ever leave me. I'm sure of it." She watched to see what Sheila was going to pull out of her purse.

"Well, before you do anything else with Richard, I wish you would discuss it with your therapist." She stopped searching for a moment and crammed her half-eaten Big Mac back in the bag along with her empty fry box.

"You're not going to finish your sandwich?" Kim asked.

"I lost my appetite." She began to search her purse again. Finally, she came up with a photograph, and she slid it across the table to Kim.

Kim picked it up. It was Sheila's husband, Damon with a very, young slim woman. "So, this was the woman you told me about," Kim said after staring at the photograph for several moments.

"That's her," Sheila responded. Her voice quivered a bit.

Kim could tell she was holding back tears. She slid the photograph back to her. "I didn't mean to upset you so much. Don't worry before anything else happens between Richard and me, I will talk to Dr. Ball. I'm seeing her after I get off work today."

"I thought you saw her on Wednesdays after work. Today is Monday." Sheila returned the picture to her purse and grabbed the last dry napkin to dab a tear or two from her eye to stop any potential full-blown waterworks.

"We had to reschedule. She has some sort of business meeting this week on Wednesday."

Sheila cleared her throat to demonstrate that she had regained her composure. "Good. You need to see her as soon as possible. Now, let's go back to work."

22

Kim walked into Dr. Ball's office at about 5 pm after leaving work. She felt anxious about her session today. She knew that when she took Sheila's advice to tell Dr. Ball about the kiss she shared with Richard, she would not approve.

"Hi, Dr. Ball." She took her regular seat on the sofa and watched Dr. Ball grab her yellow legal pad and pen. She plopped into her office chair and rolled toward her in her usual manner. The smell of vanilla air freshener and mint tea soothed her a bit. Dr. Ball pressed play on her recorder. She tried to relax, but Dr. Ball's voice, deep and authoritative, put things even more out of balance. "Hello to you. Now, let's dive right in. I'm anxious to hear about the date with the police officer you met at work."

"James?" Kim asked. She rubbed the sweat from her palms on her champagne-colored skirt, then pulled the sides of her matching jacket together to cover her red low-cut blouse. She saw the disapproving glance Dr. Ball gave her.

"Is that his name?"

"Yes. The date went well." Kim declared.

"You went to a company picnic, right?" Dr. Ball placed a pair of glasses that hung from her neck up to her eyes and wrote something down.

Kim started to fidget with her hands. "Yes," she answered.

Dr. Ball handed her a purple stress ball. "Squeeze this. It will help relieve some of your anxiety. Was there any chemistry?"

Her hands felt a bit cramped from the mountain of reports she'd been typing at work. Her muscles relaxed a bit at the feel of the spongy ball in her hands as she contemplated how she would answer Dr. Ball's question. Seemed that was the same question that had ignited the fiery exchange with Sheila earlier at lunch. "Lieutenant Kemper kissed me!" Kim blurted out.

"Lieutenant Kemper?" Dr. Ball looked confused.

Kim jumped up from her seat on the sofa and began to pace the floor. She tried to continue squeezing the ball, but she didn't seem to be able to pace and squeeze the ball at the same time.

Dr. Ball kept facing the sofa as if Kim were still sitting there.

"My boss. Lieutenant Kemper. The married man. The man in my dreams. The one you warned me to stay away from." Kim rattled the descriptions off in a defiant tone as she paced the floor frantically.

"Is he interested in starting an affair with you?" Dr. Ball crossed her leg and spun a bit in her chair to look at Kim. The question seemed condescending.

"He told me that it should never happen again." Kim rubbed the owl that sat on Dr. Ball's desk as if she hoped that she might gain wisdom from it—not wisdom about her desire for Richard, but wisdom about how to rationalize that desire to Dr. Ball so that she could make *her* look like a fool instead of feeling like one.

Dr. Ball spun her chair back around to the sofa as if Kim had returned to her seat and began writing notes again. "Well, he's right about that, but how do you feel?"

"I want to pursue a relationship with him. I had that dream about him for a reason, and I've got to pursue it if he's interested."

"Kim, that's a dangerous move for a fragile person like yourself. You are barely over this guy, Len White that you told me was the reason you moved here from Columbus. You told me that you want a man that can commit to you. It's very unlikely that a married man will give you the kind of relationship you want. Besides, it's not good for you to get involved with someone you work with either. Please, think this through a little more. Try to give things a little more time before you get involved with anyone. You need some clarity."

Kim moved a couple of steps from Dr. Ball's desk and the owl. She stood behind Dr. Ball's chair and looked down at her hair, admiring the slight streaks of gray while breathing in the aroma of violets, which made it seem as if she were the flower itself. She wore a violet-colored suit with an expensive pink silk shell that complemented her dark skin nicely. She looked warm and wise, sitting there with so much composure. She reminded her a bit of her mother.

"I'm lonely," Kim whined. "I have to do something with my time."

"Well," Dr. Ball spun her chair around to look directly at Kim. "Do you have any hobbies you've been neglecting?"

"I don't want a hobby! I want a man!" Kim screamed.

Kim noticed how the wedding ring on Dr. Ball's finger sparkled as if to taunt her. Dr. Ball placed her pad and pen on the sofa and got up from her seat. "Would you like to join me in a cup of tea? It's very relaxing." Her voice, still calm, seemed unaffected by Kim's outbursts.

"Sure," Kim answered in exasperation. She walked over to Dr. Ball's office window and looked out over the parking lot of the medical building on Euclid Avenue, just a few minutes from her home—her arms folded tightly across her chest.

"Kim, I can't tell you what to do as you have already made that painfully clear to me on a couple of our earlier sessions. Nevertheless, I can't in good conscience neglect to tell you my opinion about your decisions." She went over to the counter in her office, poured hot water from a coffee pot that was heating on the coffee maker into two white mugs, selected a tea flavor and placed a bag in each mug.

"That's what my health insurance pays you for," Kim said as she sighed with disdain and turned away from the window, forcing herself to let her arms fall to her side, realizing that she couldn't comfort herself. She needed someone else to do that.

"If you must be with a man, at least pursue one that's not married. Why don't you continue to see this police officer that took you to the picnic?" She handed Kim one of the mugs. "Sugar?"

Kim nodded in the affirmative. "He's Lieutenant Kemper's brother."

"Well, that does present a problem." She handed Kim a few packets of sugar and a spoon and continued, "However, it might deter you from pursuing your feelings for Richard if you dated his brother."

Maybe James can give me the comfort I need, and he is available, Kim thought. *But, before I make any commitment to James, I have to make sure that I have absolutely no chance of winning Richard away from his wife first!*

"I'll think about it," Kim said as she took a sip of the tea and returned to her seat on the sofa.

Dr. Ball rubbed the wooden owl that decorated the top of her desk as if she was hoping it would give her the right words to say, "You do that."

23

⌒⌒∽

Kim grimaced as she turned the television off after watching an episode of Fatal Attraction on TV One. She couldn't believe the woman would actually kill her husband just because he didn't do everything perfect. She would kill to have a man liked the one that woman killed. He adored her. He married her. He was faithful to her, and she was mad because he wasn't perfect—mad enough to kill him. When a woman has a good man, she never appreciates him; and when a man has a good woman, he never appreciates her. *Why did it always have to work out that way?* She finished the pasta salad that she had for dinner. It was just after 9, and she wondered if it was too late to call James. She wanted to know if he knew why Richard didn't come to work today.

She thought about how much Dr. Ball wanted her to pursue a relationship with James instead of Richard. Well, since Richard was married, why shouldn't she see James as a front to get to know Richard before she got in too deep with him? *That would help with appearances at work, with Dr. Ball, with Sheila, and with anybody else who wanted to stick their nose in where it didn't belong*, she thought.

She picked up her remote control to let Maze featuring Frankie Beverly play softly, while she talked to James. The drum beat followed by the guitar line and Frankie's scatting for "While I'm Alone," emanated through her Bose system speakers as she picked up her cordless landline and punched in the numbers to James' cell.

"Hello Beautiful," he said when he picked up.

"Hi. How are you, Handsome?" she replied. She picked up her cell phone and started to look at a photo she had of Richard from the Memorial Day picnic.

"Great, now that I hear your voice."

She liked how he was always shooting game. "It's good to hear your voice, too." She told him as she noticed that his voice wasn't quite as deep or as soothing as Richard's, but it was smooth.

"That's not all you're gonna like," he bragged.

She smiled at his confidence as she continued to swipe through photos of Richard. She stopped at another one that they took together at the picnic. "Is that right?" she responded to James.

"That's right, Beautiful. What made you call me tonight?"

"I didn't wake you, did I?" She enlarged the picture to where all she could see is Richard's face.

"No, I don't usually turn in until the day is over."

"Oh, it's not over for you yet?" She silently kissed her finger and placed it on Richard's lips.

"The day ends at midnight as far as I'm concerned."

"I'm calling because you asked me to call you if I was interested in going to dinner with you tomorrow evening."

"To be honest, I didn't think you'd call," James admitted.

Kim stared into Richard's eyes. "Why?" she asked as she got up from her comfortable position on the red leather sofa and walked over to the stairs.

"Well, I felt something was going on between you and my brother."

"Really?" She tried to sound concerned as she began her ascent to the top of the stairs.

"Yeah, but I know that's crazy because no one loves his wife the way my brother Richard loves Janice."

Kim frowned. She tried to stay encouraged by remembering the kiss they shared. "Does he love her enough to take a day off to play?" she asked, barely able to disguise her disappointment at hearing James' words.

"They've been known to play hooky from work, school, or whatever to get their freak on!" James laughed. "But lately," he continued. Then, he stopped in mid-thought.

"Lately, what?" Kim urged him to continue.

"Nothing," he answered.

"I hate that!" Kim walked into her bedroom and began to pace the floor. The reds and blacks of the décor mirroring her internal conflict. The reds revealing the passion she felt for Richard as well as the anger rising at James' words. The blacks showcasing the loneliness and despair she felt at having such an unattainable goal that she so desperately felt was her destiny.

"Hate what?" James asked. His sounded worried.

"I hate when people start to say something and then, leave you hanging!" Kim threw her cell phone on the bed and began to search the drawers of her red armoire for her nightshirt.

"Well, don't get mad. It's just that what I was about to say really wouldn't be right for me to share. I don't tell any of my brothers' personal business, and they don't tell mine."

"Well, is it too personal to ask why Lieutenant Kemper wasn't at work today?" Kim pulled a black nightshirt from the drawer. She put James on speaker and began to shed her clothing.

"No. I'll tell you at dinner tomorrow. We'll leave straight from work. Is that okay?"

"That's fine," she agreed.

"Good. I'll catch a ride to work with my partner, and if you don't mind, you can drive us to the restaurant in your car and bring me home after our date."

"You sure got me doing a lot." Kim teased as she pulled the black nightshirt over her head and plopped onto her queen-sized bed.

"I've got to make sure that you're the right woman for me." He teased her back.

You're definitely 'not' the right man for me, Kim thought. *Not if I can have your brother.* "So, I'll see you tomorrow," she told him as she slipped under the covers and picked up her cell to look at Richard's picture again.

"Tomorrow it is," he replied.

They both hung up, and Kim turned over, hugging her cell phone with Richard's picture tightly against her heart.

24

"Kim, can I see you in the office, please," she heard his voice and could feel him peeping his head out of the office door as she sat with her back to him typing reports.

Kim couldn't imagine what he wanted to discuss with her. She had a lot of reports to file, and even though, she loved any excuse to be around him, she was anxious to get her work done. When she walked into the office, it had been totally transformed. The desk was covered with a black tablecloth, a vase with a single red rose in the center. He stood with his back to her as he stared out of the large picture window out at the city's skyline as he often loved to do.

"Help yourself to some chocolate-covered strawberries," he told her.

"Can we do this now?" Kim asked as she reached for a strawberry.

"We can do whatever you're willing to do." He walked around the desk and moved in behind Kim as she reached for the second strawberry.

"Are you ready for this?" he whispered in her ear.

His breath was hot on her neck, and she knew she was more than ready. "Yes," she whispered.

She tensed when he began to kiss her neck and nibble on her ear.

"I can pour you a glass of wine to loosen you up if you need it."

Kim nodded in the affirmative, and he reached both his arms around her body to pick up the Moscato and the wine glass. He poured two glasses. He handed one to Kim as he continued to kiss the back of her neck gently. They sipped the wine between the kisses he planted softly on the nape of her neck, her back and her ears—never allowing her to face him.

He unzipped the red form-fitting dress she wore and eased it off her shoulders, letting it drop to the floor. She stepped out of her red pumps as he continued to kiss her.

"Are you sure we can do this here?" she asked. She could feel his eyes admiring her body adorned in only a black lace bra and panties.

She could feel his erection against the back of her thigh. She was impressed by his size. She closed her eyes and immersed herself in the moment.

"We're already doing it," he whispered. He backed a few steps away from her. She heard him lock the office door. Then, he closed the blinds that allowed him to look out into her office.

"Yes, we are," she moaned as he rubbed himself against her again.

He caressed her breasts while kissing her shoulders and neck, "How's that feel?"

"You know I love it," she moaned.

He unsnapped the bra, and it fell to the floor. Then, he picked up the remote control to the stereo. He hit a button and LTD's "Love Ballad," filled the room.

Kim smiled as his hands caressed her hips firmly before sliding her panties down her thighs and legs onto the floor, he went to the floor with them on his knees. He did things with his tongue that she never experienced before. She screamed so loudly, she was sure that the whole Justice Center had heard her.

"You like that?" She heard him whisper.

All she could do was nod her head as he bent her over the desk, and she felt him move inside of her from behind and began thrusting in and out as gently as he could. All the while, he held her waist with one hand, caressed one of her breasts with the other and whispered how good she felt between kisses on her back, arms and shoulders.

She couldn't believe how good he felt. He was truly the man of her dreams. She tried hard not to scream out again so loudly. She just knew that someone was going to come rushing in to catch them, and they would be fired.

As if he read her mind, he whispered, "Don't worry about anything, Beautiful. Just stay focused on loving me because I'm not thinking about anyone or anything else but you." The comfort of his words and his voice melted everything in her heart and soul. She immersed herself in the moment, in his words, in his love-making, in his presence. Before she knew it, she was screaming again. He didn't try to quiet her. "That's right, Beautiful. Let it go," he whispered as he began to moan in ecstasy.

"Richard! Richard!" she screamed as she awakened from the dream. Her bed was soaked with moisture. She looked at her alarm clock. It was 5 a.m. Time to get up and go to work.

25

Kim was impressed with the ambience of the Cedar Creek Restaurant in Beachwood as James pulled out her chair, and she sat down, looking around at the white tablecloths, black napkins, and red accents. It reminded her of her own apartment. She loved the mix of those colors—the red that inspired the passion in her, the black that touched the parts inside her that were so lonely that at times she didn't want to go on, and the white that contrasted the black, assuring her that hope was near. Fresh chocolate-covered strawberries added to the color scheme as the aroma caressed her nostrils, reminding her of the gentleness of the love-making she enjoyed in the dream from last night. The smell of wood-fire and grilling steaks toasted the atmosphere, giving Kim a warm, cozy romantic feeling.

"So, how'd you enjoy our first date at the company picnic?" James asked as he picked up the menu to decide on an entrée.

"I enjoyed it a lot," Kim answered, remembering the kiss she'd shared with Richard. "So, you promised to tell me why Richard hasn't been to work."

"You're not going to start our first romantic date talking about my brother, are you?"

Kim smiled. She knew she had to make James believe that her true interest was in him. "I just wanted to know how I should proceed with his cases without him there."

The server arrived. "Can I get either of you a glass of wine or some other beverage?" she asked. Kim noticed that James looked at her a little too long for her tastes. The woman was somewhat attractive, but her uniform of black slacks and a white button down shirt wasn't alluring in the least.

"What would you like, Beautiful?" he asked.

"A sparkling Moscato will be fine," she answered.

"We'll both have a sparkling Moscato," he told the server, turning his attention back to Kim.

"Turquoise and brown complements your complexion," he said. Kim wore a turquoise, brown and white print sleeveless dress with a short brown jacket that matched the brown in the dress.

"Thank you. Brown looks good on you, too," she told him and took another eyeful of his form-fitting brown muscle shirt. He wore khaki slacks that she'd checked out when he had met her in the parking lot at work. *He must have changed out of his police uniform in the locker room.* "I feel like you watched me get dressed this morning."

"I hope to do that someday, soon." James winked his eye at her.

Kim blushed.

"So, whose the fool that let you get away?" he asked as he took a swallow from a glass of water.

"Len White," Kim said before she even thought twice about the answer she would give him. "And who was your fool?"

James smiled. Kim observed that his teeth were as white as the restaurant's tablecloths. She smiled with him. "I get the feeling that question has a double meaning."

"Just answer the question. I answered it for you," she teased him as she buttered a dinner roll.

"Pam," he answered. His voice was quiet. He looked down at his hands that he rested in a folded position on the table. "Pam Jackson." Then, he lifted his glass of water again, but this time he gulped the water as if he needed it to keep from making himself vulnerable in the conversation.

"She certainly took the bravado out of your voice!" Kim said as she took a bite of the dinner roll and enjoyed its warmth and softness. It blended with James' company nicely.

The server returned with two glasses of wine. "Are the two of you ready to order?"

"Do you know what you want?" James asked. He looked relieved that the server had interrupted their conversation.

"I'll have chicken alfredo," Kim responded.

"I'll have the filet mignon with a baked potato," he told the server.

"Sour cream and butter?" The server smiled more at James, Kim thought. She twisted her lip as she watched James smile back.

"Yes," he answered her.

"And how about you, Ma'am?" Kim laughed a bit at the maroon lipstick that smeared her top two teeth. Had she not been flirting with James, she might have told her about it. *Serves her right for looking at my date*, Kim thought, and it pleased her to let the server walk around with stained teeth, smiling so generously at men who were on dates.

"I'll have Italian dressing for my salad, please." She looked at James who was staring back at her.

"Me too," he said, flashing his radiant smile at her. Then, he glanced at the server again as she walked away.

Kim thought he was looking at her behind. "What happened to Pam? Did she leave you because you're a player?" She took a sip of the wine.

"You think I'm a player?" James' voice went up at least an octave.

"Yes, I think you're a player!" Kim imitated the high pitch screech in his voice.

"I'll admit it. I have my way with the ladies, but I'm thinking about settling down. I give you credit for that."

"Me?" Kim asked in surprise. The server returned and placed their salads on the table. Kim immediately started to dig in.

"Yes, you." He glanced at the server again as she walked away.

"I can't tell by the way you keep checking out that server," Kim confessed.

"Old habits die hard. So, tell me about this Len."

"There's nothing to tell. He was married."

"You think you'd like to see me again?"

"I don't know. I have to be honest with you. I have feelings for someone else."

"Len?"

"I don't really want to talk about it. Let's just see how dinner goes."

26

Richard heard someone hurrying down the steps into his man cave. *Who dared to enter 'the man cave'?* He asked himself. He knew that his family knew better. His man cave was his sanctuary furnished with a pool table, his 60' inch flat screen, black leather sofa and chairs, a refrigerator, and a table and chairs for playing games and cards. The doors to the laundry room and the bathroom were light wood with gold door knobs. The walls were off white trimmed with light wood, and the carpet was beige. The room featured lots of wood, leather, dim lighting and neutral colors, and Janice kept it immaculate.

He looked up from the Cavs' game to see that the footsteps came from none other than his brother, James, who sat on the black leather sofa next to him without speaking and took a bite of his pizza that was cold now since he had ordered it before the game, which was now in the last few minutes of the second quarter.

"What brings you here?" he asked. He wasn't very happy to see James, but of course, he didn't want him to know it. *Janice must have let him in,* he thought. She must be back from working out at the YMCA. He was so focused on the game, he supposed that he hadn't heard her come in. She went every Tuesday and Thursday evening so he and the boys would eat fast food on those evenings.

"I need to talk," was James' cool response.

Richard muted the game and gave his brother a questioning gaze.

"This is cold as hell!" he shouted after he bit into the pizza and put the slice back into the box.

Richard gave him a stern look, thinking, *Damn! Your inconsiderate ass just bit my last slice of pizza!* "Where you coming from?" he asked his brother, trying to avoid snapping his head off.

"Oh, I just had dinner at the Cedar Creek," he said as he focused on the game.

Richard folded his arms and bit his lip. *I should knock this Negro up side his head. Taking my last slice of pizza, and he just got through eating!* "So, what do you need to talk about?" he asked James.

"You gotta make that!" James yelled at the television when Timofey Mosgov missed a dunk. "Where are the boys?" he asked, settling back into his seat.

"In their rooms," Richard answered him, feeling exasperated by the fact that he was taking so long to get to the point of his visit.

"Your secretary is wondering why you haven't been to work," he said when he glanced away from the television and caught Richard giving him the evil eye. "What do you want me to tell her?" He smiled at seeing the Cavaliers winning score at the end of the half.

"Tell her the truth—that I have an assignment in Detroit for the next few weeks. She can have Sergeant Brown sign off on my cases until I come back."

"I'll tell her," he said. After a few moments of silence, the brothers both staring at the television screen, James finally got to the point of his visit. "I think I'm falling for her." His comment was nonchalant as he leaned forward in his seat and rested his elbows on his lap.

"James, you don't fall for women." The words were more Richard's hope than his true belief. Kim was so sexy.

He could definitely understand why James would be getting serious about her, and she had this willingness to please that a lot of women just didn't possess.

"It's something about her," James continued.

Richard felt as though James read his mind, and he was annoyed that his brother would make this announcement at a time when he had to be away from the office. He thought about the kiss he and Kim had shared at the picnic. Since the picnic, and except for his health, he wasn't able to think about anything else.

"So, I take it since you took that assignment in Detroit, the doctors gave you a clean bill of health?" James inquired.

"Yes. I'm good. They couldn't find anything wrong with me. So, they told me to take the week off. I plan to stay at home for a few days to rest. Then, I'll head out to Detroit to work on this case. They prescribed some pain killers for my headaches. They said I just need some rest from the stress at work."

"You need some sex." James laughed and propped his feet up on the cocktail table.

Richard looked at his sandaled feet with envy. *He must the only man I know that gets pedicures.* "You ain't lying about that!" Richard agreed with his brother and remembered the kiss again. "So, you really serious about Kim?" He held up a bottle of beer that he'd been drinking in a gesture to offer one to James. "You just met her."

"I know, but no one has made me feel like this since Pam." He nodded in affirmation to Richard's gesture about the beer.

"What? No, you're not bringing up Pam! You haven't mentioned her since you guys broke up." He got up went to the refrigerator, retrieved another bottle of beer and tossed it to James.

"Well, you know I'm trying to forget about her."

"And you think Kim will give you Pamnesia?" Richard asked as he resumed his seat on the sofa next to James.

"I know Kim will give me, as you call it, Pamnesia."

"Well, I guess you should go for it, then." Richard couldn't believe that he let those words come out of his mouth. Then, he reasoned to himself that he couldn't pursue anything with Kim. He had to step aside for his brother.

"I would, except, she told me that she has feelings for someone else."

Richard sat up straight. He couldn't help but wonder if this other man she had feelings for was him. "Feelings for someone else?"

"Yeah," James admitted.

"Who? Did she tell you?"

"She mentioned some guy that she was dealing with in Columbus. His name is Len. That's all she told me."

Richard let go of his breath. James gave him an inquisitive look. "What's with you, Man? Are you okay?"

"I'm good. It's just that it seems this situation that you've gotten yourself into with my secretary is a bit intense. I hope it doesn't affect her work or our relationship."

"How would it affect your relationship with her?"

"If you guys don't work out, she'll be a problem at work. I just know what's gonna happen!" Richard took the mute off the sound just as LeBron hit a three-point shot.

"Yes!!!" the brothers shouted as they both jumped to their feet and slapped a high five.

Richard scorned himself inside for trying to dissuade his brother from a woman that he obviously was developing real feelings for just because he lusted after her.

"Man, you gotta do what you gotta do," he conceded as they took their seats again, letting their hearts settle as it looked as if the Cavs were going to be the Eastern Conference champions by the end of the game and go to the NBA finals for the first time since 2007.

"How's things with Janice?" James asked as he took a swig from the bottle of beer.

"Everything's fine," he lied.

"So, she's giving it up like you like it?"

"Man, I don't want to talk about our sex life with you!" He got up to toss his empty beer bottle in the trash and went to the fridge to get another one.

"So, you're still frustrated." James laughed. "I tell you between you, Anthony and Junie, I don't know which of you are getting the least. You make marriage seem like it's a sex cemetery."

"I'll have you to know that Janice and I have had almost two decades of great sex. It's just something's different now. I want something different."

"It sure wouldn't take me twenty years to get tired of the same thing." James laughed again and took the last swig of his beer.

"See that's why you need to leave Ms. Nelson alone. You're just going to kick it with her until you get tired and move on. Then, she'll be giving me the evil eye at work every time she thinks about how dirty you did her."

"I think I can get used to monogamy with a woman like Kim." James got up from his seat and went over to the fridge to retrieve his second beer.

"Don't make me regret it if you pursue a relationship with her, or believe me, I'll get you back."

"Don't worry, Man. I got this!"

They clinked beer bottles, took a swig of beer and looked up at the television screen as the final seconds ran off the clock, and the Cleveland Cavaliers were declared Eastern Conference Champions.

27

"Richard! What are you doing here?" Kim asked as she let him into her apartment.

It was a great question, he thought because he had no idea why he had decided to just suddenly show up at her apartment. He liked her décor. The red, black and white colors spoke to him about her passion, loneliness and hope as if they were characters in a movie. He longed for her passion. He, too, was lonely, and she seemed as if she held his only hope of feeling alive again.

"I need to talk to you—about my brother," he added because that's what he'd just decided was the reason for his visit.

"What about James?" she asked, offering him a seat. He sat in her white leather recliner, and she sat on the red leather sofa.

"I don't know if it's a good idea for you to see my brother after what happened between us," he stated.

"Why? You told me to never bring up our kiss again. You said it was a mistake. You said that you were happy with your wife. You're confusing me."

"It just feels messy." Richard repositioned himself in his seat, trying to get comfortable. He felt out of place in Kim's apartment. He watched her as she picked up a remote control, pushed a button, and in the seconds, he was listening to "Happy Feelings" by Maze featuring Frankie Beverly. He was impressed that a woman in her thirties could appreciate old school R&B. Most people their age liked Drake and Nikki Minaj.

"How can it be messy if we never mention the kiss again?" Her lips dripped with red gloss that complemented the red silk pajamas she wore. The pajamas were the sexiest he'd ever seen—the top had spaghetti strings for sleeves and was low cut with lace at the cleavage. The bottoms were short and showcased her beautiful caramel-colored thighs. He wished that she would put on a robe or something.

"My brother told me that you told him that you weren't sure if you would continue seeing him because you have feelings for someone else. I don't want you to hurt my brother."

"I'm sure your brother can take care of himself," she told him, appearing unaffected by his concern for his brother. She moved to the corner of the L-shaped sofa and stretched her legs across it with her back sitting against the end of it. "Sexy, confident guy like James has probably left a nice trail of broken hearts. You should have seen the way he checked out the server when we were at dinner."

"If you hurt my brother, you'll answer to me."

"And who are you going to answer to, if *you* hurt him?" She gave him a look that beckoned him to join her on the sofa.

He felt himself getting aroused at the mere thought of being close to her. He cursed himself. "I'm not doing this!" He stood to his feet.

She stood, too. "What Richard? What is it that you're not doing?" She stood directly in front of him.

"I'm not going to cheat on my wife with you, and I'm not going to get in this messy triangle between you, me and my brother."

Kim put her arms around his waist. "I think you want me, Lieutenant."

Richard felt himself rising and getting harder. He had to have her, he thought. *No! He had to get out of there*, he thought better. She grabbed his hand and caressed it, brought it to her lips and kissed it. Her lips felt soft, wet and inviting. He imagined that being inside of her would feel even better. He wanted to beg her to have mercy on him and just stop touching him, but he didn't want to admit how weak he felt. He didn't know how he was going to overcome what he was feeling and get out of her apartment. He should have never come to see her. He knew she could feel him throbbing against her. He loved the feel of her red silk pajamas as he began to caress her. He tried as hard as he could to push Janice in her yellow negligée out of his mind.

"I can't do this, Kim. I love my wife."

Kim stepped away from him. "If you love your wife, then why are you here?"

"I told you. I'm concerned about my brother."

"You're lying."

"Why are you so sure that I want you?"

"I just felt how much you wanted me against my thigh. Are you gonna keep denying it?"

"You're sexy. I admit that, and *he* might want you," he said looking down at himself. "But, *he* doesn't have any sense. So, I don't do everything *he* tells me to do. If I did, my marriage would not have lasted all these years."

"The attraction between us is real and it's destined to happen. I know it." Kim moved away from him and headed into her kitchen. Richard followed her with his body and eyes, but his feet stayed planted where he stood.

"That's impossible. I can't risk losing my wife and family just because you give me an erection."

"I dreamt about us before I even met you. We are meant to be together. I know it." Kim opened her refrigerator and retrieved two bottles of water.

"You're talking crazy. I don't know what you dreamed, but I know I'm going to do whatever it takes to keep my family together. I don't care how sexy you are."

"Richard, don't come to my house playing games with me. If you don't want me, don't tease me. Just leave!" She tossed him a bottle of water. "And maybe you should pour that on your erection!"

28

Richard was glad to be back home. What was he thinking? He should have never gone to Kim's apartment. He had come so close to sleeping with Kim and destroying his marriage, he didn't even want to think about it. His wife had to stop freezing him out. If he didn't make love to her tonight, he didn't think he'd be able to resist Kim much longer.

He entered their bedroom, and she was reading a novel by author, Deborah McDaniel. He noticed the title, "What You Do in the Dark." He grimaced just thinking about what he almost did in the dark, and he knew the rest of that saying meant nothing but trouble for him.

"Hey," he said to her.

She looked up. "Oh, you're home. I didn't know you were going out. The doctor said he wanted you to get some rest. Are you sure you should be exerting yourself like that?"

"I'm okay, but I'll take it easy this week. I promise if you'll promise me something."

"Sure. I'll promise you anything if I thought it would keep you with me and the kids for a few more years." She smiled and closed the novel.

"I'm going to be gone for about two or three weeks when I take this assignment in Detroit. Are you going to miss me?"

"You know I will. When do you leave?"

"I'll probably drive to Detroit on Sunday afternoon and have dinner with my brother, Junie and his wife." Richard went into their walk-in closet, took off his clothes and came back into the room in black boxer briefs. When he looked at Janice, she was reading the novel again.

"What's so interesting about that book that you can't give your husband your undivided attention?" Richard frowned as he walked over to his side of the bed.

"What is it, Richard? Why are you acting so irritable? You know I always read in bed before I go to sleep."

"We have to fix what's broke between us, Janice. It's crucial." He looked over his shoulder as he stood with his back to her, preparing to sit on the edge of the bed. He noticed she was wearing a gray T-shirt. It aggravated him. She never even tried to appeal to him sexually anymore.

"What's wrong?" she asked.

He couldn't believe that she didn't even notice that he was struggling sexually. They'd known each other since they were kids, but he was starting to feel as if they didn't know each other at all.

"You don't take care of me anymore." He sat down.

"You don't take care of me anymore!" she shot back.

"Janice, we can't keep doing this." He turned halfway toward her and looked into her eyes.

"What is it, Richard?" She softened a bit.

He felt a bit encouraged. "Janice, you know I love you, and I love our kids. I love our life."

"Yes. I do. So, what's wrong?"

"We haven't been together. It's been so long since you've even touched me, and then, we were in the middle of making love the last time, you just abandoned me to help Sonny do his homework."

"Richard, I had to help him."

"And what about me, Janice? Who's gonna help me?"

She crawled from under the yellow, gray and white comforter and sheets and wrapped her arms around Richard's neck and kissed him on the cheek. "Baby, you seemed so stressed. I guess I didn't realize, I've been neglecting you."

Richard reached for her hand over his shoulder. She hugged him tightly with her other arm and continued to kiss his neck. He could feel how much she loved him.

"I need you, Janice."

"I need you, too, Richard." She hugged him tighter. He could feel a few tears drop from her face onto his shoulder.

"I mean I really need you." He stood and faced her, revealing his erection through his black form-fitting boxer briefs. She pulled his underwear down just enough to kiss him. He moaned with appreciation.

He was so happy that his wife was pleasing him again. He stood there immersing himself in the warmth and softness of her mouth, but before he knew it, he was thinking of Kim. The shame overtook him, and he started to go limp. Janice looked up at him with confusion in her eyes. He sat on the bed next to her and kissed her lips. He decided to please her orally instead, but he didn't really enjoy it. He moved his tongue to the rhythm of her body movements and responded to her moans, but his heart wasn't in it. All he could think about was how much he would rather be giving pleasure to Kim.

It seemed like hours passed before he heard Janice scream out in ecstasy that indicated she had reached an orgasm. He went to the bathroom to rinse his mouth with Scope. As he swished it around, he felt himself get aroused again as he thought about Kim. He decided that when he went back into the bedroom that he would just penetrate Janice, get his orgasm and go to sleep without trying to think about it too much.

Yet, when he returned to the bed, Janice was passed out. He shook her, but all she did was snore. He was so mad, he could have spit. He needed to relieve himself so badly, he didn't know what to do. He went back into the bathroom to take a shower and have yet another encounter with his hand as he thought of making love to Kim.

29

Devastated by his performance with his wife the night before, Richard didn't even want to join his family for dinner. He decided to leave home for a long drive. He found himself at the Longhorn Steakhouse in Solon, Ohio. When he walked in, he couldn't believe who he saw sitting at the bar.

"Can I join you?" he asked.

"Shouldn't you be at home with your family?" Her form-fitting two-piece red suit looked remarkable on her curvaceous frame as always.

"Do you have a date with my brother? Are you waiting for him? Or can I buy you a drink?" Richard admired how her soft caramel-colored skin reflected against the glow of the dim lighting in the restaurant with its dark woods and rugged décor. The light conversations of the patrons in the bar area provided a soothing background and made him feel a lot less stressed than he'd felt in days.

"I just stopped by here to have a bite to eat after work. What's your excuse? Are your wife and kids meeting you here? I thought you were supposed to be home resting."

"Sometimes you just need to get away from it all," he told her as he summoned one of the servers to take his order. "What are you drinking?"

"I'll have a sparkling Moscato," she declared.

"I need something a little stronger," he admitted. "Would you get the lady a sparkling Moscato, and I'll have a gin and ginger ale."

"I'm sorry for getting angry with you yesterday. You have every right to want to remain faithful to your wife. I don't know what I was thinking."

"It's okay. I led you on."

"You're admitting that?"

"I am. I can't deny it. I want you."

"So what are you going to do about it?"

"I don't know. I don't think my feelings for you are going to just go away. I just don't want to hurt my wife or my brother. Are you going to keep seeing him or not?"

"I don't know."

"Kim, I can't do this to my brother." The server placed their drinks in front of them. Richard quickly picked up his drink and downed it in almost one gulp. "Did you say you're having dinner?"

"Yes, I'm waiting for a table." She held up the buzzer that the restaurant gave her so that they could notify her when her table was available.

"Can I join you?"

"Sure, but what about your wife, your kids, your brother?" She crossed her leg.

Her caramel-colored thighs caught his eye. He imagined himself between them. He immediately wanted her again. He thought about how he couldn't keep his erection for his wife because of her the night before. "Just for tonight, let's just forget about James, Janice and everybody else. I want to get to know my new secretary."

"That sounds like a plan," Kim agreed and she licked her lips. They were glossed with red, and they looked wet, soft and inviting. He imagined the lips between her legs would offer more of the same.

He wished that he could get his mind off of making love to her. "So, I want hear about this guy, Len that sent you running here from Columbus."

The buzzer lit up, and they followed the hostess to their table that was near the rear of the restaurant—dark, secluded and cozy. He watched as Kim slid into the booth, and he slid in on the other side facing the door.

"I'd been involved with Len for almost a year. I thought we were in love. I can't believe how stupid I was. I mean he could never spend any weekends with me—no holidays. He always said he had to work, and I believed him."

"So, he was married?" Richard nodded in the affirmative when the server asked if he wanted another gin and ginger ale.

Kim still sipped from her glass of wine. "Yes," she admitted.

"So, you like married men?"

"No. It just seems that's who I keep meeting."

"Well, you know they say that the definition of insanity is doing the same thing over and over again, expecting different results."

"Are you calling me crazy?" She stuck her lip out in a sexy pout. Richard wanted to kiss it.

"Are you?" He folded his arms, and he stared Kim down with his interrogation eyes that he'd used on so many criminal suspects in homicide investigations.

"Well, I see a therapist. Does that make me crazy?"

The server brought Richard's drink. He gulped it down without answering Kim's question. "I'd like a grilled chicken dinner with mashed potatoes and green beans," he told her.

"I'll have shrimp linguini," Kim said. She licked her glossy lips again.

Richard repositioned himself to try to achieve some comfort from how she made him feel. "You come to a steakhouse to have linguini?"

"You come to have chicken?"

"Touché," he said. He drank some of the water the server had left on the table. "I have to admit that I think you're sexy. Do you like working for me?"

"I love it. Hey, who's your favorite female musical artist?" she asked him.

"I love Diana Ross. Who's your favorite male artist?"

"I love Lionel Richie."

"Can you sing?" He watched her take the last sip of the Moscato.

"A little. Can you?"

"A little. I think we should go to Karaoke and sing "Endless Love," Richard suggested.

"When?" She took off her suit jacket, and she had on a low-cut black shell underneath it. Her cleavage peeked over the edge of the blouse in a seductive, enticing manner. His eyes focused involuntarily.

"After we eat." He heard his voice tremble with emotion.

"I have a better idea." She smiled at her plate as the server placed it in front of her.

Richard wished the smile was for him. "What's that?" he asked.

"Let's go bowling. I discovered that there are some really nice lanes right around the corner from here—Freeway Lanes."

"Bowling!" He couldn't imagine why she would suggest that over Karaoke.

"Bowling is fun, relaxing, and I know you have a competitive spirit. We can place a wager on our games."

"I know you're not suggesting that you can beat me in any sport." Richard started to cut his chicken and put a forkful in his mouth as he imagined that the strings of linguini hanging from Kim's mouth was pleasure that she'd provided for him.

"What do you want to wager?" Kim asked, biting into a piece of bread.

"You can call it," Richard conceded, knowing that the only thing on his mind was making love to her. He knew he would suggest something totally inappropriate.

"If I win, you spend the night with me," she said.

"You're a bit forward, aren't you?" was the question out of his mouth, but his member was screaming "Yes!"

"Richard, if you want me, and I want you, why don't we give in to what we want? You only live once."

"Problem is, the stakes are much too high, but I'll accept your wager because I know you can't beat me bowling." He took another bite of the chicken.

"Okay. So, what do you get if you win?"

"You stop seeing my brother." He took a drink of water as he almost choked at hearing his bold request.

"Wow! You play hard. You got a deal, Lieutenant Kemper."

"Now, tonight I want you to call me Richard."

30

They laughed at a joke Richard told as they changed from their own shoes into bowling shoes. Richard could hardly wait to watch Kim bowl with that red skirt rising up in the back every time she bent over to lunge the ball down the lane. As it was a Friday night, the lanes were filled with patrons, mostly league bowlers. Richard had worried that they might not be able to secure a lane, and he worried more that someone from the police department might be there. As luck would have it, a few lanes were available, and he didn't see anyone he knew.

"So, how'd you find out Len was married?" he asked as he set up the electronic scoring for their game. He was a bit annoyed that he had to shout in order for Kim to hear him as the noise level of the lanes was loud with laughter of all types, trash-talking filled with profanity, pins falling as they were hit with full force by balls weighing 8-16 pounds moving at lightning speed and hitting their targets with crashes that sounded like thunder.

"I went to our favorite restaurant, and there he was with his two children." Kim moved close to him so that they could lower their voices.

"I imagine it must have hurt to discover that you've been caught up in someone's web of lies," he said as he placed the red bowling ball he'd found on the rack, raising his voice again.

Kim placed a black ball on the rack, "Hurts like hell," she admitted. "I tried to commit suicide." Her voice was barely a whisper.

Nevertheless, due to her close proximity, Richard heard her loud and clear. "Because of a loser like that?" He was disgusted that someone as beautiful as Kim would let a man have that much power over her happiness.

"I think it was more because of you," she shared.

"Me?" He went to bowl, and he knocked down a strike. He pumped his fist in a gesture of triumph as he returned to their seats. "You might as well delete my brother's number from your phone right now!"

She walked up to the lane and took her turn. She only knocked down five on the first try, and then another three. "It was the dream that made me want to die."

Richard looked confused. "The dream?"

"Yes. Remember, I told you I dreamt about you before I met you. I came to your office, and you were standing there, looking out over the skyline. The next thing I knew, we were making love, and you said that I was going to be your wife."

"You had this dream before we met?" He got up and headed to the lane. This time he only knocked down three pins. He heard a guy a couple of lanes over yell, "Strike!" "How do these people expect you to be able to concentrate with them yelling like that," he complained.

Kim smiled. "No excuses." She got up from her seat and headed to the lanes. Richard couldn't wait to sit down and watch. She didn't disappoint. The back of her thighs were so smooth and inviting, he throbbed with desire.

This was a bad idea, he thought. He was glad he'd taken that assignment in Detroit. He had to get a handle on his attraction to Kim. Somehow, he had to get her out of his system, out of his desires, out of his dreams.

"Your turn," she told him as she returned to her seat.

He looked up at the screen and noticed that she had gotten a strike. He had to beat her. If he could get her out of James' life, then maybe he could have a little bit more control over how much interaction he had with her. He wished he didn't have to work with her, but he couldn't fathom going another few weeks without a secretary again while they tried to find a replacement for her. He lunged the ball down the lane and hit a strike.

"Hey, how about I get us a couple of drinks from the bar?" He started to head toward the bar to order.

"That would be great. Just get me a wine cooler or something," she told him. He paused to watch again as she took her turn. When she bent over, he forced himself to look away.

After three games, Richard took two and Kim one. "I guess I'll have to break your brother's heart," Kim announced as she changed her shoes.

Richard slid his feet into his sneakers. "Don't do that. You're right. My brother would be heart-broken."

"So, what do you want me to give you for beating me?"

He watched as she slipped her smooth, beautifully pedicured feet into her red high-heeled sandals. "I just need you to respect my marriage."

Kim frowned. He could tell that he had disappointed her. "No problem." Her lips were in a pout again, and it was all Richard could do to not kiss them.

"You'll love James. All the ladies do."

"I don't want James! I want you!" she yelled. Other patrons at the lanes turned to look at her. Richard hoped no one recognized him.

"Kim, coming here with you tonight was a mistake. I have way too much to lose to be playing this game with you. You have to understand that. I love my wife!"

"Who are you trying to convince? Me? Or yourself?" She stormed out of the bowling alley. He walked swiftly to keep a safe distance behind her. He watched as she got into her car.

"I'm sorry," he whispered to himself as he watched her speed off.

31

Kim stood at the big picture window in Lieutenant Kemper's office reflecting on her dream about making love to him in this office. She missed him. He'd been out of the office now for a week. She wondered if she should continue to see James considering how she felt about his brother. It was crazy to keep pursuing him when he'd made it crystal clear that he was devoted to his wife. She started to understand why Sheila and Dr. Ball were so frustrated with her for insisting that she and Lieutenant Kemper were destined to be together, but they just didn't understand the power of that dream. No man had ever made love to her the way Lieutenant Kemper did in that dream. She didn't care if he didn't leave his wife. She just wanted to experience him one time.

She placed the reports she'd been holding on Lieutenant Kemper's desk as Detective Henderson entered the office. "You got the report on that evidence I requested yesterday?" he asked, standing in the door.

Kim looked up at him. He had smooth, milk chocolate skin, a nice build, bald head, and full lips. "Of course, Detective Henderson, you know I wouldn't let you down." Kim admired the way his broad shoulders and thick arms filled out his navy blue uniform.

"That's great," he said with a smile and he folded his hands in front of him, which made his wedding ring more visible.

Kim brushed past him to exit Lieutenant Kemper's office, entering her adjoining office, to retrieve the report he wanted from her desk. She handed it to him. "Here you are, Detective."

"You're doing a great job in the big man's absence. I'll be sure to tell him when he returns."

"Thank you, Detective Henderson. I would appreciate a good word."

"Good word about what?" Detective Bobbie Johnson suddenly appeared and placed a report on Kim's desk.

"I was just telling Ms. Nelson, she was doing a great job."

"Yeah, you are. You almost make us forget about Anna," Detective Johnson stated. She was short, stocky, but attractive. Her breasts just about busted out of her uniform. She wore her hair in a neat French roll, and her hands were manicured, but her nails were cut short. "It's nice to be appreciated," Kim said as she sat down to type the report that Detective Johnson had just put on her desk.

"Did you pick up that report on the murder weapon we needed?" Detective Johnson asked her partner.

"Ms. Nelson just handed it to me," he answered.

"Great. Let's go take a look at it." They both smiled at Kim as they left.

Kim liked her new job. She stood for a moment to look at the picture of President Barack Obama and Vice President Joe Biden on the wall. She didn't realize it when she worked as a legal secretary in Columbus how much better it would make her feel to be on the side of the good guys. In Columbus, she looked at her work as just a way to make money, but now she was living her dream. She was using her skills to help the police convict criminals. The only thing that she didn't like was the scrutiny that the police were under with regard to brutality against African Americans.

She was glad that she worked with mostly African American police detectives and that her supervisor was an African American lieutenant. The black community didn't really blame them as much for all the killings of the scores of African American males in the past few years as they did white police officers.

Her thoughts turned to Lieutenant Kemper and her dream when the ringing telephone interrupted them. "Lieutenant Kemper's office," she said when she picked it up.

"Hey, Girl. It's me, Sheila. What you doing for lunch?"

"Nothing. You want to go to the Galleria?"

"Sounds like a plan. How's it going for you, working without the man *of* your dreams...I mean *in* your dreams?"

"I miss him."

"I bet you do. Are you going to take my suggestion and continue to date James and try to forget about him?"

"Maybe."

"I'm telling you, Girl. You need to take my advice. You will be so much happier. I really don't want to see you get hurt again. Lieutenant Kemper is a family man, and he loves his wife. You don't want to break up a happy home, do you?"

"Sheila, it's just that the dream was so real, and it felt so good. I'd be happy just to be with him if only for just one night."

"Alright, Luther Vandross. I'm telling you…I don't care how good it seemed in that dream, it's not worth destroying that man's marriage, your reputation, and possibly even your job. The whole thing is just so unethical, unhealthy, and unforgivable."

"Well, Sheila. I'll try to stay away from him. It's easy now that he's away from work for a while, but I can't make any promises."

"I'm gonna pray for you."

"And by the way, you didn't tell me about James' reputation with the ladies. I don't think he's any better for me than Lieutenant Kemper."

"At least he's single," Sheila replied.

Kim could hear the indignation in her voice. She wanted to call her best friend out for being a hypocrite, but she knew that Sheila was more than ready to do battle in order to convince her to abandon her dream of having a relationship with Lieutenant Kemper—even if it meant that she got involved with a player like James. "I'll see you at noon, Ms. Sheila." She always addressed her this way when she was annoyed with her friend, but didn't want to argue.

"Okay. See you then."

32

It was close to lunch time, and Kim had just one more report to type. She hurried to get it done, but between the telephone ringing and detectives coming in and out requesting reports, she didn't think she'd get it done before lunch. She knew she had two more reports coming for the afternoon, and if she could get the one done that she was typing, she'd have just enough time to get the afternoon reports done before 4:30.

"Hello, Beautiful," a sexy voice greeted her.

She stared into a firm abdomen covered with a navy blue uniform, which fit its muscular body like spandex. She looked up at his golden oak complexioned face as a seductive, chalk white smile oozed from between his bronzed-colored lips, and his light brown eyes intensified by his dark brows and hair, peered into hers.

"Oh. Hello, James."

He pulled a bouquet of white chrysanthemums from behind his back. "Would these flowers convince you to join me for lunch today?"

Kim was impressed. She couldn't remember when the last time she had received flowers from a man. She stood to look them over. "They're beautiful," she told him. She tried not to smile too much, but it was so difficult to contain her excitement. She perused the cabinets in her office until she found a vase. Then, she placed the flowers inside.

James went over to the counter to the coffee maker. He made two cups of coffee and handed one to Kim. "So, you didn't answer me about lunch."

"I made plans to have lunch with Sheila, and I have to finish this report before I leave, and I only have about ten minutes."

"You're not really going to turn me down, are you?" He moved closer to Kim. He wore some kind of earthy fragrance like a musk cologne. Kim thought it was intoxicating.

"What am I going to do about Sheila?" she protested. She tried to step back, but there was no room to move away. She fell back into her chair. James broke her fall with an embrace. His lips were so close to hers, she was sure that he was going to kiss her.

Instead, as he stared into her eyes, he asked "Am I making you nervous?"

"I'm okay, but I think you need to let me go. We're in the workplace, you know."

"In the words of Snoop, if you scared, go to church." He laughed.

Kim laughed, too. "That's so corny, James."

He stood straight and folded his arms. "Let's go to lunch," he said. His tone was firm.

Kim thought about Sheila's words of encouragement for her to date James. She knew that if she broke their lunch date to be with James, she would not mind at all. "Let me call Sheila."

Kim picked up the phone to call Sheila. James walked into his brother's office.

Once Kim broke her lunch date with Sheila, she followed James into Lieutenant Kemper's office. When she entered the office, he was standing in front of the picture window the way Lieutenant Kemper often did—just staring at the skyline.

"You miss him?" she asked.

He turned and looked at Kim. "Of course," he answered. "But, he'll be back soon."

"He will," Kim whispered.

"Come here," he beckoned with his arms.

"James, we're at work," she protested.

He walked over to her, and took her hand. He guided her to the window. "Do you like it here in Cleveland?" he asked as they stood and stared at the skyline together.

"I was just thinking about that."

James moved behind her and put his arms around her waist. "Richard and I like looking out over this skyline because it makes us feel powerful."

"Why? Do you imagine you own the town or something?" Kim asked.

"We protect and serve this city, Ms. Nelson. That's an awesome responsibility."

"I suppose it is."

"You know I have a dream," James shared.

"Okay, Dr. King." Kim laughed and continued to look at the skyline.

"I would love to make love to you in this office with that skyline staring at us. I want to protect and serve you, too."

"You're talking like you've got a thing for me or something, Mr. Kemper."

"I am starting to feel some type a way about you, Girl."

"James, the player, starting to feel something for a woman!" Kim teased him. "Are you serious? Or is this how you get a woman hooked by making her believe you really feel something for her?"

"I've always been real, Kim. I don't lead women on. I don't have to do that. My game is just that strong."

Kim took in his fragrance and felt the hardness of his abdomen against her back. She knew a lot of women wanted him. She smiled at this words. She had to agree. He definitely didn't have to tell any lies to get a woman. "Is that right?" She finally responded.

"You know I'm telling the truth. Now, let's get out of here, my lunch break will be over soon. So, if you're not going to let me make love to you on my brother's desk, I suggest we get out of here."

I'm never going to make love to you on this desk, Kim declared in her mind. She had a flash of her dream and vowed to herself in that moment. *If I make love to anybody on this desk, it will be your brother.*

"Let me grab my purse," she told James as they prepared to go to lunch.

33

Kim was so tired when she got home that evening, but she felt good about her lunch date with James. She couldn't believe that she had accepted another date with him for dinner. She had to admit that she loved the attention that he gave her, but she didn't believe she could let go of her attraction to his brother.

She plopped on her red leather living room sofa and kicked off her green sandals. She wanted to lay down for a moment before she showered and put on her form-fitting black dress for her date with James. It was 5:15 James said he'd pick her up at about 7. So, she decided to take a fifteen minute nap.

The phone rang about four times during her restless nap. Each time she looked at the caller ID, it was Sheila. No doubt, she wanted to know how things went on the lunch date. "I'll tell you when I get home tonight!" she shouted to the ringing phone as she dragged herself upstairs to her bathroom for a shower.

By 6, she had finished her shower and was pulling her black dress over her freshly oiled body. She shook her jet black weaved locks onto her shoulders and checked her reflection in her full length mirror. She heard her door buzzer and cussed James for coming early.

She skipped down the stairs and walked over to the intercom, "You're early!" she yelled into it.

"I didn't know I had an appointment," a familiar voice answered her.

She buzzed him in, and went to the door. Standing with her arms folded, she asked "Len, what are you doing here? How did you find me?"

He walked through the door and headed to her sofa to take a seat. "I talked to your mother." He sat on the sofa, leaned back and made himself comfortable.

Kim looked at him with scorn. "I can't believe she didn't warn me." She picked up her phone and scrolled her missed calls, and there it was, three missed calls from her mother.

"You don't seem like you're happy to see me." He crossed his legs in a triumphant gesture.

"You think," her words reeked of sarcasm. "How's your wife?"

"We're divorcing," Len announced.

Kim watched him as he adjusted the collar on his light blue polo shirt and rubbed his hand across his goatee. His sexy smirk endeared him to her in spite of her feelings. "Is that right?" She spat out the comment as if it were venom.

"That's right." He smoothed his starched khaki pants.

"And this concerns me how?" Kim sat in her white leather recliner and crossed her legs at the ankles, bringing Len's attention to her bare feet and long silky legs—and a peek at her healthy thighs.

"You have dinner plans?" he asked.

"I do," she responded in a matter-of-fact tone.

"I'm here because I wanted you to know that I still love you, and I want you back as soon as my divorce is final if you'll have me."

"Len, are you serious? I live in Cleveland now. I moved to get away from you. To start over. I'm not coming back to you. I'm happy."

"You were happy with me." He got up from the sofa and walked over to the chair where Kim was seated and knelt at her feet. Then, he kissed her thigh.

"What are you doing?" She crossed her leg in an effort to stop his advances.

He went into the side pocket of his khaki pants and pulled out some papers. He handed them to Kim. When she took them, he kissed her thigh again as she read them. They were divorce papers. "Give me another chance," he pleaded. He kissed her knees. Then, he lifted her leg and put her big toe in his mouth.

Flashes of their lovemaking filled Kim's head. She remembered that he was a very good lover. She felt herself melting at his touch, but then she heard his son ask, "Who is that lady, Daddy?" and his answer, "Nobody, Son."

"Stop it! I'm not doing this with you again, Len!" She squirmed to get away from him.

They both stood. "Kim, forgive me. You won't regret it. I promise." He embraced her and kissed her neck.

"How can I ever trust you, Len?" She tried to pry herself from his grasp.

"If you give me a chance, I'll earn your trust again. Just give me a chance. That's all I ask. What we had is worth that, at least. Isn't it?"

He continued to kiss her neck. She could smell his cologne—Obsession. She remembered the day they'd gone shopping together in Macy's and decided to by the female and male versions of the cologne. Whenever, he wore it, she was mesmerized. She could feel his desire for her. It enticed her. She couldn't deny that she wanted him again, but she couldn't forget all the pain she experienced when she discovered his lies. He was so good at lying.

"Why?" she managed to force the question from her lips between his gentle kisses.

"What you talking about, Baby?" he asked as he began to lick her cleavage.

"Why did you lie to me about your wife and kids? Why didn't you just tell me the truth?"

"I don't know, Baby. I didn't think I'd have a chance with you if I didn't."

The door buzzer rang.

"Len, I have a date. You're going to have to leave." She pushed him away and went to the intercom. "Yes!"

"It's me, Beautiful. Buzz me up!"

"Len, you'll have to leave. He's on his way up." Kim opened the door and gestured for Len to leave.

"I know you don't want me to leave," he told her, and he moved closer to her and began to kiss her again. "I love you. I can't leave."

Kim melted when he told her that he loved her. She forgot that James was on his way to her apartment. She began to kiss Len back. They moved to the sofa. He pushed her down on it and got on top of her, running his hand under her dress and pulling down her black lace panties, kissing her thighs, her stomach, teasing her. She moaned and begged him to please her. He lifted her thighs high and rested her legs on his shoulder as he kissed her between them.

34

"Wait, wait!" Kim screamed. "We can't do this now. You know my date is on his way to my apartment."

Len let Kim sit up and put her underwear on.

"Am I interrupting something?" James said as he walked in, holding a bottle of wine and another bouquet of white chrysanthemums.

Kim jumped up from the sofa and straightened her dress. She stared at the white of the modest flowers and felt a twinge of guilt. The fresh green stems contrasted nicely with the mint green Polo shirt James wore that complemented his hunter green knee length shorts. Kim liked how he put his outfits together, and she recognized his cologne as Guess Seductive. Feeling like she was in the middle of seduction and obsession, her knees felt weak.

"Wow! You look amazing," James told her.

She wanted to return the compliment, but she felt a bit unhinged by the fact that she was still tingling from Len's tongue. "Uh, James this is Len White. He came to visit me from Columbus."

"Oh," James said. He put the wine on the dinette table and walked into the living room area to present the flowers to Kim. "Is this the guy you told me about?"

Kim felt her voice tremble when she answered, "Yes. Maybe we should reschedule our date." She took the flowers from James.

"Nonsense, Beautiful. We can give your out of town guest a little taste of Cleveland. He can join us."

Trying to think of a reason to protest, she said, "James. I don't know."

"Would that be okay with you, uh—Len, is it?"

"Yes." Len answered.

"Good, let's go."

"Well, I meant…" Len tried to correct his answer.

"Hey, Man. Chill. I'll show you guys a great time." James assured them.

"I need to finish getting dressed," Kim told him.

"You do that, Beautiful. I'll keep your friend company." James took a seat in the white recliner, while Len made himself more comfortable on the red sofa.

"Well, at least let me pour you guys a glass of wine before I leave the two of you alone. James, it was so kind of you to bring it. It's my favorite, Seven Daughters."

"You're welcome, Beautiful. My parents raised me well," he said. Then, he flashed a look at Len, observing the table as if he were looking for something that Len had brought.

Kim took the flowers with her into the kitchen, put them in a red vase and placed them on her dinette table.

Len leaned back on the red leather sofa and spread his legs wide with his arms across the top of the sofa in a triumphant pose.

"You have a nice place, Kim," James said, looking around at the red, white and black décor.

"Is this your first time here?" Len asked.

"Kim is the kind of woman you have to respect and take your time with," he shared. "And, you have to be honest with her." He winked his eye at Len.

Len popped some mints in his mouth that he'd retrieved from the glass cocktail table. Then, he began to play with the white decorative pillows.

James picked up the remote to the television and turned to the NBA finals game.

Kim brought them each a glass of wine, and asked, "Will you guys be okay while I finish getting myself together for the evening?"

"You look fine the way you are, but I'm a big boy. I can handle myself." James took the glass from Kim and took a sip.

"Well, you know that I know that you do need to freshen up, Sweetheart. You got another bathroom in here? I could stand to throw some water in a couple of places myself," Len added. He gulped a big swallow of his wine, and returned James' wink.

Kim gave Len a look of scorn. "If either of you need to use the restroom, there is a half bath just off the kitchen. I'll be right back." Reluctantly, she left the men alone and went upstairs to freshen up from her close sexual encounter with Len. She wanted to put on her high-heeled black sandals with the silver rhinestones, grab her silver handbag, and touch up her makeup. She couldn't believe that she'd almost had sex with Len again. As a matter of fact, she wished she could get rid of James so they could finish what he'd started. He was about to rock her world! He felt so good, she almost didn't care that James had almost caught them.

Nevertheless, she knew she couldn't possibly pick back up with Len. He lived two hours away. What if she wanted him in the middle of the week? She didn't believe she could do a long distance relationship. She smiled at the memory of seeing those divorce papers as she spread red lip gloss generously across her lips. This could be the answer to everything. If she went back to Len, she wouldn't have to worry about coming between the Kemper brothers.

She left her bathroom mirror and entered her adjoining bedroom to sit on her bed. She slid her pedicured feet into her sandals, taking her time as she didn't know if she was ready to be with the man who wanted to be her future and the man who was her past at the same time.

"You stupid ass!" she heard Len shout from her living room.

"Oh, no!" she thought. "They're fighting," she whispered. She wondered what she should do. Should she call the police? Go downstairs and try to stop them?

"What an asshole!" James shouted back.

She couldn't just hide out in her room. She had to go downstairs and stop them from arguing.

"Ain't that a bitch?" Len hollered.

"Mother---!"

"James!" Kim shouted as she reached the last step.

"Yeah, Beautiful. You ready?"

"What's going on?" Kim surveyed James carefully.

He stood next to Len with his arms folded. "These refs are full of sh--!" They both looked as if they were about to pounce on the television at any m-oment.

"James!" Kim shouted to interrupt his verbal assault.

"I'm sorry, Beautiful. These refs are about to cause the Cavs to lose the game!" he yelled.

Kim realized that they had not been yelling at each other, but instead, they were shouting at the television. She was so embarrassed that she thought that they were fighting over her.

"You got any beer?" Len asked.

"Beer!" Kim shouted with indignation.

Both men sat on the sofa. They didn't look like they were ready to go anywhere.

"Yeah, a cold beer would be nice," James agreed. "And some chips. You got any chips?"

"We should just order a pizza," Len suggested.

The men slapped each other a high five. "Now you talking, my brother!" James laughed as they both focused on the game.

"What about giving Len a taste of Cleveland?" Kim asked.

"Yes!" the men shouted as they jumped to their feet when LeBron hit a three-point shot to give Cleveland the lead.

"Now, Baby. What better way to give him a taste of Cleveland than to let him enjoy a Cavs game in the comfort of your beautiful home? And if you order some Angela Mia's pizza, well that will give him all the taste he needs."

Disappointed, frustrated, but obviously out-numbered, Kim kicked off her sandals, and made the call to Angela Mia's.

35

It was 10 am Saturday morning when Kim stormed into Dr. Ball's office and took her usual seat. Her white summer dress spread like daisy petals against the black sofa. The yellow of the walls sickened her more than usual. She stared at the wooden owl on Dr. Ball's desk, and wondered if she really had any wisdom at all when it came to helping her with her issues.

"Dr. Ball, what is the purpose of our meetings?" she asked with fire in her eyes and anger in her heart.

"What would you like the purpose to be?" Dr. Ball asked as she took a seat in her office chair and rolled it close to Kim in her usual manner. She positioned herself with her yellow legal pad and pen. Then, she pressed play on her pocket-sized recorder.

"I want to have a healthy romantic relationship with a man. Is that what you are trying to help me do? Or are you just trying to get me to be happy being alone?"

"Kim, I can only help you with the things in your life that you can control. So, I'm not here to help you find a man. I'm here to help you deal with any man you might decide to start a relationship with in a healthy manner. I want to keep you in a place where you want to live a long, full life. I want to help you battle depression. Are you still seeing James?" She crossed her legs and sat back in her chair ready to write notes.

Kim thought she wanted a long monologue about James and Richard again. "Yes," she answered, refusing to cooperate.

"How's that going?" Dr. Ball asked.

"I don't know. Len came to visit me. He's getting a divorce, and he wants me back."

"Is that what you want?"

"I want Richard."

"And, you want Richard because you still believe that he's the man in your dreams?"

"You're finally starting to get the picture, Dr. Ball." She spat out the sarcastic response like it was phlegm caught in her throat.

"Oh, yes. I've got the picture," Dr. Ball said with her own hint of sarcasm.

"Don't patronize me. You're getting paid to help me—not make fun of me."

Dr. Ball got up from her seat, and went over to the counter where she kept her beverages. "Would you like some tea?"

"Not today." Kim felt eager to get into a meaningful discussion. She didn't want to calm down, which she knew was Dr. Ball's purpose in offering the tea.

"You know I've done quite a bit of work in dream interpretation," Dr. Ball said as she poured hot water into a cup to make tea for herself and stirred in some sugar. She looked strong and empowered as she stood at the counter wearing a two-piece violet suit and matching shoes. Her white shell juxtaposed against her dark brown skin gave Kim a sense of hope.

"Good for you," Kim responded. She crossed her legs and arms in protest. She admired her own French-pedicured feet in white sandals.

"I thought you might like to explore your dream today."

"How would we go about that?" She let her arms fall to her lap, admiring her French-manicured hands. Then, she felt a twinge of regret at seeing the emptiness of her third, left finger after comparing it to Dr. Ball's same finger.

Before Dr. Ball returned to her seat, she watered a cactus plant on her desk. Kim felt as one with the plant—prickly and green with envy as she squinted at the sparkle of Dr. Ball's wedding ring. The marquise cut of the diamond made her ache with longing for the day the man of her dreams would propose to her on one knee with the black velvet box in his hand, opening it just after he declares his love for her along with the fact that he can't imagine his life without her.

"Well, I want you to tell me the details about the dreams, and we're going to pick out some significant objects and ideas from it, and I will tell you what they usually mean. But, what I want you to focus on is what those objects and ideas mean to you."

"I guess it couldn't hurt anything. So, the first thing I remember is that every time I see him for the first time, he's standing in his office in this big picture window, looking out over the city's skyline."

Dr. Ball wrote some notes. Kim tried to see what she wrote, but Dr. Ball's hand was in the way—and that ring continued to glisten in her face, reminding her of her single status.

"Well, let's look for a moment at the fact that you keep recognizing that the man is looking out at the city's skyline."

"Okay." Kim sat forward. She felt more intrigued by the idea of dream interpretation than she wanted Dr. Ball to know, and she was eager to do anything to get her mind off of the fact that she seemed such a long way from marrying the man of her dreams.

"Dreaming about a city skyline could reveal a longing to be a part of city life or a desire to outline something. It also could represent boundaries, perspectives or convergence. Lastly, it could reflect a feeling that it is time to get distance from something."

"That's interesting," Kim stated. "I came to Cleveland to get distance from Len. I needed a new perspective on life."

"I think it's interesting, too, that you needed to get distance from a man, but the man is looking at the skyline. It might mean that the right man is looking for you."

"Richard is the man," Kim said with conviction.

"Is Richard looking for you? Or are you pursuing Richard?" Dr. Ball asked. She crossed her leg in a triumphant posture.

What was she trying to prove? Kim wondered. "It has to be Richard. It's Richard's office."

"Well, next week, why don't we explore what the office means in your dreams? I'll do some research between now and our next meeting."

"Okay," Kim agreed.

36

Richard was glad to be able to enjoy a Saturday evening at home. Things were still tense with Janice, so he spent the day in his man cave. He was tired of watching movies so he decided to practice his pool game. Just as he racked the balls, he heard a barrage of footsteps descending upon him. He wondered if it were his sons. They hadn't hung out with him all day, but what could he expect. His oldest was starting to take an interest in girls. Sonny would much rather hang out with his mom when he wasn't practicing his basketball skills, and his namesake loved to play video games with his best friend, AJ.

"What's up Rich?" James said as he entered first wearing jeans and a gold Cavs T-shirt.

His twin, Johnny, followed him wearing jeans and a gray Cavs T-shirt, "Oh, I see you're preparing for a beat-down!"

Anthony was last, "Not if I'm on his team!" He wore a plain white T-shirt with his jeans.

"Let's do it," Richard loved to wear mesh shorts and tanks. He rubbed his hands against the gray of his tank top when he challenged the twins and welcomed his older brother to his side with a hearty hug and handshake.

"Break'em," James responded to Richard's challenge.

Richard handed his brother Anthony a cue stick. The twins retrieved their own. Anthony broke the balls, and hit two shots immediately back to back.

Seeing James reminded Richard of his attraction to Kim. He wondered if he was getting anywhere with her, but he didn't want to ask. Fortunately, James took care of it for him.

"Man, your secretary is giving me the blues," he started.

Before Richard could say anything, Anthony jumped in, "A woman? Giving you the blues?" He hit his third shot.

Johnny laughed. "Am I dreaming? Or did I hear 'Playa-playa' say a woman was giving him the blues? Ain't no woman gave him the blues since Pam!"

The other brothers got quiet, and they gave Johnny a look as if to say, *You know you ain't supposed to bring up her name!*

Anthony missed his shot. Johnny leaned over the pool table quickly to take advantage of the miss.

"You heard right," James said. He held his cue stick in a vertical position on the floor, and he let his eyes follow its length to the top as if he were looking up at a tall building.

"What's going on?" Anthony asked.

"Yeah. I gotta hear this," Johnny said after he hit his first shot.

"Well, we had a date. It was our second. I go to pick her up for dinner, and this guy she's been talking about from Columbus is there."

"Wow! So, how did you handle that?" Anthony asked as he watched Richard take a shot. Johnny had just missed.

Richard missed. He couldn't concentrate. He was a little flustered at hearing that, not only was his brother competing with him for Kim's affection, but so was that old flame from Columbus that she'd told him about.

"Damn," Johnny said. "Where's your game, Rich?"

Richard sat on a stool in the corner, while James took his turn. He hoped that it would take a while for his turn to come around. He wanted to concentrate on James' story. He waved Johnny off—not even taking the opportunity to brag on what he was going to do the next time it was his turn.

"Damn his game!" Anthony shouted. "Let's get back to this woman, Kim, and her giving the notorious player of the family the blues."

Richard wanted to give Anthony a high five on that proclamation, but instead he just made himself a little more comfortable on his stool and waited for James to get on with his story.

"So, go on. Tell us how you handled this other guy showing up," Anthony urged.

"Well, she tried to cancel our date, but I told her that we could all go out."

"What?!" Johnny and Anthony hollered.

"Yeah. She went upstairs to finish getting dressed, and the next thing you know, we're watching the Cavs' game and bonding like boys." James' hit his shot and pumped his fist in triumph.

"So, you made friends with her ex?" Johnny asked.

"Pretty much," James admitted as he hit another shot.

"You the man!" Johnny exclaimed, slapping a high five with James.

"Yeah. Only problem is I got the feeling the guy was trying to let me know that he had banged her—like recently," James shared.

Richard didn't know how to digest that information. He felt glad that it seemed his brother was doing a good job of getting Kim's ex out of the picture, but now Richard wondered how he could get James out of the picture. And, had he really gotten the guy out of the picture—seeing as though he thought they had been screwing.

"Come on, Rich. Where are you? It's your turn," Anthony told him.

Richard got up to shoot and missed again.

"I don't know why the hell I chose you for a teammate," Anthony complained.

"How's things going with Janice?" James asked.

"The same," Richard answered, returning to his seat.

"Maybe you guys should take a vacation," Anthony suggested. "That might put the spark back in the bedroom."

James hit the eight ball in and called, "Game!"

"So, Rich? You gonna take Anthony's advice?" Johnny asked.

Richard didn't want to talk about his marriage. "You guys want a beer?" he asked instead of answering Johnny's question.

He went into his man cave fridge and got them all a beer as they prepared to watch a NBA Finals game on his 60' flat screen television.

37

$\sim\!\!\infty\!\!\sim$

After the game, his brothers left, and Richard found himself parked in front of Kim's apartment. He sat there for what seemed like hours just staring at the apartment building, wondering if he should go to the door.

He searched the playlist on his I-pod and chose Ashford and Simpson's "It Seems to Hang On." He must have let it play about five or six times, while he relaxed in his 2014 black Chevy Impala. Before he knew it, he was singing with it until there was a rap on his car window—the Euclid police.

Richard let his window down, "Yes. What can I do for you officer?"

"Someone called complaining that a man has been sitting in front of this apartment building for an hour."

Richard asked, "Can I show you my ID? I'm a lieutenant for the Cleveland Police Department. I don't mean anyone any harm. I just arrived too early to meet a friend so I'm waiting for him to arrive."

"I noticed the police decal on your plates, but we have to check things out when we get a call," the officer replied. He was a young white officer. Richard deduced that he probably hadn't been with the force long.

Richard reached inside his glove compartment and pulled out his wallet. He showed the officer his badge, and the rookie saluted him like they were in the Army. Then, he returned to his black and white and drove away.

What are you doing? Richard asked himself. *Are you stalking your secretary? Well, since you're here, you might as well see if she'll let you in. But, what if James shows up? He won't. He said he was tired and was going home to get some sleep.* Richard found that hard to believe, though. James never went to bed this early on a Saturday night. He listened to Ashford and Simpson one more time, mustered up all the courage he could, and got out of his car.

He headed to the apartment lobby and buzzed Kim's apartment.

"Hello," he heard her voice. He got aroused immediately. He couldn't believe how much he wanted her.

"Hi. It's me, Lieutenant Kemper," he announced.

"Mr. Kemper? What are you doing here?"

"I need to talk to you about my brother."

There was a long pause. He shuffled his feet. *Was she going to let him in? And if she did, what would he say about James?*

Finally, the door buzzer clicked to unlock the entry door. He went inside, and her door was cracked. He entered. He saw a red leather sofa with white pillows and a white leather recliner, but he didn't see her anywhere. He took a seat in the recliner. After a few moments, Kim descended the stairs, wearing a black lace nightie with a black silk robe. She had on black-heeled slippers that showed off her French pedicured toes.

He stood from the chair, "Hi," he said. He felt desire for her before she even said anything.

"Hi," she said, taking a seat on the sofa. The black of her negligée and the red of the sofa complemented each other with a mix of passion and longing that increased his desire more than he thought possible. Her caramel-colored thigh begged for a bit of ice cream and his tongue.

"So, what did you want to talk to me about?" She picked up the remote control and turned on her stereo. The sounds of Maze's "Lady of Magic" filled the room.

"Are you really into him? Or are you just playing him for this guy from Columbus?"

She smiled through the red glossiness of her lips, and he thought that if he kissed her, those moist-looking lips might taste like a candy apple. Her teeth were white like the inside of a juicy apple.

"What kind of question is that?" She had a fire in her eyes that intensified his yearning to touch her.

He squirmed a bit in his seat. "I don't want you to hurt my brother."

"James seems like he can take care of himself. Besides, I thought we'd settled all this the night we went bowling." She slowly placed her legs across the sofa, leaning back in the corner of its L-shape.

Richard could just imagine himself crawling the length of her body from her toes to her garden, taking in the scent of her sexuality and tasting the essence of her soul. He crossed his legs to try to tame the growing beast that rose like a sleeping giant awakening to the call of his insatiable hunger. Straining to control himself, he said, "James told me that you're still seeing that guy, Len. He even thinks you're still sleeping with him."

Kim stood to her feet. Every curve of her body mesmerized him as he surveyed the way the lace of her black negligée fit her form, revealing the beauty of her soft, silky skin. "Mr. Kemper, I fail to see what any of this has to do with you."

"I agreed to step aside for my brother, but I won't stand by and let you screw some other man behind his back."

"Even if that other man is you?" She walked passed him and headed into the kitchen.

He caught a whiff of her perfume. She smelled shower fresh, and she looked like a sex goddess. He shouldn't have come to her apartment again. In that black negligée, she reminded him of a black widow spider. He knew he was caught in her web of seduction. He just had to have her, he thought.

"Would you like to join me in a glass of wine?" she called from the kitchen.

"Did you have sex with Len?" he asked. He hoped that she would say yes. Then, he would probably be angry and turned off.

"I certainly would like to have sex with you," she answered. She was standing beside him now with a glass of wine to offer him.

As he went to take the glass, he noticed his hand trembled at her statement. He thought it would be such a relief if he would just stop trying to be a faithful husband and succumbed to her advances. Janice never had to know—neither did James. *What would it hurt to just be with her once?*

He took the glass and gulped down the wine. He watched her walk over to the sofa, take a seat and a sip of her wine. Then, she sat the glass on the table in front of her as she resumed her position across the length of the sofa.

"Wine should be sipped—not gulped," she told him as she leaned back against the corner of the sofa again, gazing at him as if she admired what she saw. Her smile was sincere and heart-warming.

"You are so sexy," he admitted.

"I'm a bit tired. I'm ready to go to bed. Would you like to join me?" she asked. She got up from her seat on the sofa again, walked over to him, and took his hand.

He followed her to the stairs.

When she took the first step, he froze.

"You know I can't do this. I have to get home to my wife."

38

When Richard got home, he went up to his bedroom immediately. Janice was reading as usual. He was filled with guilt and anger. Guilty because he wanted Kim so badly. Anger because his wife did not arouse him anymore.

"You're home," she said, putting down her Essence magazine. Instead of yellow, she had on a pink nightie. She had that look of innocence that he remembered from when they were teens, and they made love for the first time. Back then, he thought she was the most beautiful woman he'd ever seen. That innocence of hers intoxicated him with desire for her, and every muscle, tendon and bone in his body would ache for her.

He undressed quickly, turned off the lamp on his nightstand, and jumped into bed wearing only his gray boxer briefs. Janice moved close to him and tried to cuddle. Guilt from his brief encounter with Kim told him to turn his back to her. *Women were so perceptive*, he thought. If he allowed her to get too close, she might smell her scent on him. He'd never survive an interrogation from Janice.

"Everything okay?" she asked.

"Yeah. I'm just tired." He grabbed one of his pillows and hugged it tight, holding it under his face.

"The doctor says that you can exert a little energy now," she reminded him.

Guilt spoke again, telling him he had better give her the attention that she was requesting or that might make her suspicious as well. He turned toward her and kissed her lips gently. He didn't feel his body respond. She began to kiss his chest, and she moved down to his mid-section. He breathed a sigh of relief that she didn't seem to smell his flirtation with adultery on his person. He thought he might enjoy the oral sex that Janice's tongue was promising him as she continued to kiss him just below his navel. His body tensed with expectancy. Then, he made himself relax so he could immerse himself in the attention that she gave him.

The next thing he knew he was thinking about Kim. Janice must have spent almost an hour trying to please him orally. Yet, he kept seeing Kim in the black lace nightie, he got so hard, he was in pain, but every time he looked down and saw Janice, he would go limp.

"What's wrong?" Janice complained after a half hour.

"I don't know. Stress, I guess," he lied.

"Well, what do you want me to do?" she asked.

"Let's just go to sleep," he suggested.

"Baby, what about me?" she whined.

The thought of making love to her really made him go limp. "I don't know if I can make love to you tonight, Janice."

"After all this complaining you've been doing about me not taking care of you! Are you serious?" she shouted.

"Baby, stop shouting. The boys will hear you."

"The whole street is going to hear me if you don't—! Never mind. You're right. Let's just go to sleep." She pulled the yellow, white and gray comforter over her head and turned her back to Richard.

Richard turned on his back and stared at the ceiling. He needed a sexual release, and his body was not cooperating. He knew that it would if he were alone, but he didn't want to go to his man cave to pleasure himself. He wanted to be inside of his wife. What could he do to sustain an erection while he made love to her? He had to figure it out. Maybe if he kept his eyes closed and pretended he was making love to Kim, he would actually please himself and her.

So, he made up his mind. He would please her first with oral sex. Then, he would penetrate her while he pretended she was Kim.

"Come here, Baby," he said to his wife.

"What do you want?"

"Let's try it again." He moved under the covers and began to kiss her between her legs. As he kissed her, he imagined it was Kim he kissed. He thought about the black lace panties, the smell of her perfume, her caramel-colored thighs. In the darkness of their bedroom, he couldn't see

Janice's thighs, but her thighs didn't feel as big, soft and inviting as Kim's. He pushed that thought away and continued to kiss her lips.

After several minutes, he heard his wife moaning with pleasure. She didn't sound like he imagined Kim would sound. He came up for air, and he whispered, "Get the remote control. Turn on some music." He wanted to drown out her voice so that he could only hear Kim's voice in his head.

But, it was too late, she was coming to a climax, and she was screaming, and he was losing his erection, the more he heard her voice. He needed to get it back so that he could penetrate her when she finished.

"Come on, Baby. Do me," he demanded when she finished. She was never much good at oral sex after she had an orgasm, but if she could just give him a few minutes, he would have to make it work.

She began to kiss his limpness, but she wasn't doing a very good job, he thought. "Come on, Baby," he urged. He felt her tongue moving very slowly and without the rhythm he needed to get aroused. He lay still and thought about Kim in the black lace nightie again, and gradually, he felt himself getting aroused.

He remembered the perfume again. Her lips dripping with red gloss. He imagined it was her lips that he was feeling. He got more aroused. He believed he was aroused enough to have sex with his wife. He turned her over and penetrated her as he continued to think about Kim. He wished that he had turned on the stereo because he was starting to hear Janice moan again.

"Ssh," he whispered.

"Harder!" she ordered him.

He wished she hadn't said that. "Ssh," he told her again.

"I want it rough!" she yelled, and he lost his erection again.

He wanted to strangle his wife. He fell onto the bed and turned his back to her, praying for sleep to come quickly.

39

He stared at the yellow of the walls that reminded him of Janice. He didn't want to think about her today. He focused on the red and white tablecloths instead and let the clanking of dishes and the murmuring of several conversations drown out the voices that tried to tell him that he should not have scheduled this meeting.

"Yes, I'll have coffee," Richard told the server as she seated him at a booth in Bob Evans' Restaurant in Beachwood, Ohio about 6 the next evening. When the attractive female server smiled at him, he figured that he must look pretty good in the wine-colored two-piece linen short set he wore. He wanted to impress her.

"Coffee? So late, Mr. Kemper?" Kim said as she took the seat across from him.

"Thanks for meeting me," he told her.

"What would you guys like?" the server asked. She seemed a bit disappointed in seeing Kim join the party. She was a sassy African American woman with a dark-complexion and a short asymmetrical haircut that had a touch of blonde color. For a moment, Richard thought Janice might look sexy with a hairstyle like that. He dismissed the thought. *I have to stop thinking about Janice!* He scolded himself.

"I'll have a roasted chicken wing dinner with mashed potatoes and gravy," Kim said.

"Just soup and salad for me," Richard told her. He was eager to turn his attention back to Kim. "You look nice." He admired her low-cut red sundress. Again, her lips dripped with red lip gloss, and her wavy jet black hair adorned her bare caramel-colored shoulders.

"Thank you. I'm liking that wine short set on you. What's that material, linen?" she asked. She slid the restaurant menu to the edge of the table and put her elbows in its place, holding her face in her hands. She stared at Richard, smiling.

"Yes. But, I didn't ask you here to discuss our attire." He slid his menu to the edge of the table as well, and looked up at the server's hair again as she returned to pour his coffee, place a glass of water in front of Kim, pick up the menus and dash off again.

"Okay. What is it that you need to see me about?" She sipped from the water through a straw, leaving her lip prints around it.

Richard imagined that she'd leave a lip print like that around a certain part of his body. "Kim, I need to be with you. I can't keep denying it."

She wrapped those luscious lips around the straw again, taking another swig of the water before she responded. "Mr. Kemper. I don't have time to play these games with you. You don't know what you want. You keep teasing me, and then, you keep saying you have to remain faithful to your wife, and you don't want to hurt your brother."

"I don't want to hurt my wife or my brother, but Kim, I can't stop thinking about you. I can't stop wanting to be with you." He looked around, hoping he wasn't talking too loud—also wanting to make sure that there was no one in the restaurant that they knew.

Her eyes pitied him. "So, what do you expect me to do about it?"

"I made a reservation at the Embassy Suites just around the corner. Meet me there." He looked around again.

She twisted her lip in exasperation. Richard wondered if he had offended her with his paranoia. "For what? So, you can get me all riled up, just to let me down?"

"Kim, I promise. I won't stop this time. I'm ready." He forced himself to stop looking around like a whore at a church revival.

The server put their drinks on the table. Lemonade for Richard. Pepsi for Kim. They both took sips.

"Your meals will be out shortly," the server assured them.

"Are you sure about this?" Kim asked after the server walked away.

"I've never been so sure about anything in my life," Richard said as he reached across the table for Kim's hand. He resolved to commit to his desire for Kim, and to hell with anybody that saw them together.

"I don't know. I've got a lot going on, and we work together. What's going to happen after we make love? Are we going to act like it never happened? Are we going to have a relationship?"

"All I can promise is that I'll make love to you tonight with everything that I am." He saw Kim's eyes light up at his words. "Does that sound good to you?"

"It sounds great," she told him.

"It will be great," he promised.

The server returned with the meals. Richard had absolutely no appetite. He just stared at Kim as she ate her chicken and mashed potatoes.

"You look so sexy when you eat," he told her.

She blushed. He smiled. It seemed that it took forever for her to eat her dinner.

He couldn't wait to get her into that hotel room.

40

When Richard arrived, he prepared for his rendezvous quickly, ordering champagne and chocolate strawberries for Kim's arrival. He sprinkled red rose petals over the bed, which featured an olive green and rust-colored comforter. He opened the similarly colored curtains so that he could look out of the window. He could hear another couple making love in the next room, and he got aroused in anticipation of his encounter with Kim. Thoughts of his wife tried to creep into his mind, but he quickly pushed them out.

He heard a knock at the door. "Come in," he said, knowing it had to be Kim. He had given her a key at the restaurant. He turned around to see her.

She walked in, and his heart stopped. Then, it started to beat so fast, he didn't know if he should keep standing or sit down before he fell.

"You came," he stated with a hint of surprise in his voice.

"Not yet." Her voice dripped with sensuality.

Richard turned on some music. He had brought his I-pod and Bose Bluetooth speaker. Hi-Five "I Can't Wait Another Minute" filled the room as he moved closer to Kim and took her into an embrace. "Let me do something about that for you," he told her.

"Please do," she whispered as he kissed her neck. "I can't believe this is finally happening."

"It's definitely happening," Richard announced as he moved so close to her that he was sure that she felt his hardness against her thigh.

"Oh, yes. It's happening." She moaned when he slipped his hand inside her panties and penetrated her with his fingers.

After she was dripping wet, he slid his fingers out, and palmed the cheeks of her behind as she turned her back to him. He unzipped the red sundress that revealed red lace underwear. He whispered to himself, "Go slow, Boy."

He had to do something to calm himself. He didn't want to ruin their love-making with a premature ejaculation episode because he was too excited.

"Let's have some champagne," he offered.

"Sure."

He motioned for her to take a seat on the bed while he poured.

The room had a soft glow from candles he had lit. The light flickered, hitting her curvaceous body in all the right places—just enough for him to see her caramel thighs against the rose petals on the bed. The fullness of her red glossy lips shimmering and beckoning him to kiss her.

He poured the champagne and handed her a glass. She sipped it in a way that just oozed a mixture of sex and elegance. He selected a strawberry from a tray. Then, he sat next to Kim on the bed and fed it to her between her sips of champagne.

He felt himself calm down a bit, and he knew that soon he could kiss her again. As the song, "Sensuality" ended, another Isley favorite, "Touch Me," played. Richard got some massage oil that he'd placed on the nightstand and began to rub the oil on Kim's shoulders.

"How's that feel?" he asked.

"Real good," she said.

"Lay down on your stomach." He gave her a gentle command.

She complied quickly. He straddled her back and began to massage her shoulders and back gently. He could feel her relax completely.

"I've missed you at work," she said.

"Now, I know you're not going to start talking about work." He laughed a quiet laugh.

"No," she promised.

After he massaged her back, he moved to her buttocks. He removed her panties and continued to massage her, giving attention to her thighs next. When he touched her thighs for the first time, his erection was so strong, it pained him.

He picked up his glass of champagne and took one last sip. Then, he gently turned Kim over on her back. He gazed at her for a few minutes, lying there anticipating what he would do next to please her, and then, he poured the contents of his glass along the length of Kim's body. She giggled as the drops of champagne wet her skin. He placed the glass on the nightstand next to the king-sized bed. He kissed her in the middle of her breasts, licking the champagne and enjoying the taste. He immersed himself in the taste and the intoxicating power of the beverage as it led his tongue to every part of Kim's body until he found his tongue licking the moistness of her femininity. Her cries and moans of pleasure filled the room, competing with the music and a couple in another room. She grabbed and held his head with a vice grip so firm, Richard thought that she would bring back his headaches. Her juices filled his mouth and mixed with champagne, reminding him of the salty rim from a Marguerita. He got high off of the pleasure he gave her.

Next, he penetrated her, moving so deep inside her, he thought he'd lose himself. At first, each stroke brought him more pleasure than he'd ever experienced, but the closer he got to an orgasm, the more he saw Janice's face. Next, he saw James' face. Then, his sons.

When he came, instead of feeling the relief that he thought he'd feel, he felt tremendous guilt, and he wanted Kim to leave.

41

Kim came home on Friday evening around 5 p.m. and began to prepare a salad for dinner. She hadn't heard from James, which she found strange. She assumed that he'd want to spend a Friday evening with her. She grilled some tilapia to go with her salad, and took out a bottle of Aquafina. She shed her purple dress that she'd worn to work and just walked around in her black lace bra and panties. She'd decided that she would put on her pjs when she went upstairs for bed.

She turned on her stereo and listened to some Gerald Levert "I'd Give Anything" was the first track to play. She plopped onto her red leather sofa and threw the white decorative pillows on the floor. Then, she kicked off her purple sandals and propped her bare feet onto her glass cocktail table, eating quickly and holding her black stoneware plate in one hand and a silver fork in the other.

All she could think about was her scheduled visit with her therapist the next day. She wondered what Dr. Ball would tell her about the significance of Richard's office in her dreams. She was starting to like James more than she wanted to, and she really felt like she needed to make up her mind about which of the Kemper brothers she wanted before she ended up with neither of them.

She hadn't heard from Len since last week. She thought about how he came so close to pleasing her before James showed up. She wondered if she would like sex with James. She finished her meal and fell asleep on the sofa.

"I'm just going to put these files on the desk. I don't want to disturb you, Mr. Kemper," Kim said as she walked into her bosses office to find him staring out of his picture window at the city's skyline.

"You're definitely not disturbing me, Beautiful," he said as he moved in behind her as she organized the files on his desk.

"Mr. Kemper!" she said, blushing.

"Don't try to act like you don't know how much I want you," he whispered in her ear and then, he nibbled it.

His tongue gave her a tickling sensation, and she giggled. "Mr. Kemper, stop! Someone might catch us."

"No one will care. They know you're going to be my wife." He raised her skirt and pulled down her red lace panties.

She leaned over the desk to receive him. She heard his pants unzip. Then, the phone rang just as he put himself inside of her.

She picked up the receiver, "Hello. Lieutenant Kemper's office."

He started to stroke her, and she almost let out of a moan, "Oh. Oh. Mrs. Kemper. He's not here. Would you like to leave a message?"

She grabbed a note pad off the desk, and he thrust into her again. "Woo!" she moaned. "I'll tell him you called Mrs. Kemper." She hung up the phone without saying good-bye.

"How's that feel?" he asked.

"Real good."

"You know how much I love you, right?"

"I know," she said, crawling on her hands and knees, mounting the desk. He climbed up behind her and continued stroking her gently, rhythmically and passionately until they came. He covered her mouth with his hand to muffle her screams of ecstasy.

"I love you, too," she told him as she collapsed on top of the desk.

The phone rang, she woke up to answer it. "Hello."

"Hey, Girl. What you doing this evening?" her friend Sheila said in an excited voice.

"Nothing," she answered, trying to come out of her sleep. She looked at the decorative black and white clock on her living room wall. It read 6:45 pm.

"You don't sound like you ain't doing nothing. Is somebody over there?"

"No, Sheila. I just woke up."

"Did you have one of those dreams again?"

"You know I did."

"About Lieutenant Kemper?"

"Yes, and oh that man is the best lover ever!"

"You seeing Dr. Ball tomorrow?"

"You know, Sheila. My dreams have some significance according to Dr. Ball, and she's helping me to figure out what they mean. I hear that disapproval in your voice. I know Richard is the one for me. My dreams are proof! You'll see."

"Look, I ain't got nothing else to say about it."

"Good!"

"Well, I have just one thing to say."

"And what's that?"

"Kim, please! Let go of any thought of being with that married man. All something like that can lead to is scandal and pain. I thought you and James were hitting it off. I think he'd be much better for you."

"Sheila, you know that talk around the job is that he's a player, and he's slept with every single woman in the department. I don't see why you would want me to get involved with someone that has that kind of reputation."

"Looks like he's slowed down a bit since the picnic," Sheila defended herself.

"I can't believe you are pushing for me to be with a guy like that."

"I didn't introduce you to him. You met him on your own and decided to start dating him. And from what I can tell, he hasn't done anything, but treat you well. Has he had you yet?"

"Sheila!"

"Well, has he?"

"No."

"And probably only because you're too stuck on his brother to give him a snowball's chance in hell. He likes you Kim. I'd just rather you kick it with him for a while than to destroy a marriage. You know karma is a bitch!"

"And what is that supposed to mean?"

"It means, you are going to get married one day, and you ain't gonna want some skank sleeping around with your husband."

"Richard is going to be my husband, and he's going to be so in love with me that he won't look at another woman. After all, look at how loyal he is to his current wife, and he wants me."

"Forget him, Kim!"

The door buzzer rang, and Kim jumped up to go to the intercom. "Look, someone's at my door so I'll talk to you tomorrow after my therapy session."

"Okay. I'm praying that doctor can talk some sense into you."

"Bye, Felicia!"

"I got your Felicia!"

They both laughed and hung up the phone.

42

Kim opened her apartment door, and James walked in. "Did we have a date tonight?" Kim asked as she watched him walk over to her living room sofa and take a seat.

"No, I just thought I'd drop by to see if you wanted some company, and I can see by the way you're dressed that you're definitely ready for my company."

Kim looked down and realized that she was in her bra and panties. "I'm sorry. I fell asleep on the sofa, and I just woke up. I didn't realize that I wasn't dressed when I opened the door. Could you excuse me while I go upstairs and throw on a robe or something?"

"I'd prefer that you keep on what you're wearing." He smiled and looked at her approvingly.

"I'll be right back," she promised. "You like Gerald Levert?"

"Yeah. This is cool," he answered as he bobbed his head to "Nothin to Somethin."

Kim felt relieved that James had arrived. She wondered if he wanted to take her somewhere or just hang out in her apartment. She ran to her closet and slipped on a purple sundress. She felt like royalty today.

She checked her hair, fingered it into place and touched up her lips with bronze gloss and joined James in the living room again.

"You look beautiful as always," were his first words when he saw her.

She liked his white muscle shirt that he wore with black slacks as well. His physique filled out the shirt perfectly. She could look at his muscles and tell that his whole body was hard and firm. "Can I get you anything?"

"I like that Seven Daughters you keep," he told her.

She went to the kitchen and poured a couple of glasses of the Moscato and joined James on the sofa. "How was work today?" she asked as she handed him a glass.

"I took today off," he said as he took a sip of the wine.

"Oh. I wondered why you didn't ask me out to lunch today."

"Oh. You just getting spoiled. You think you supposed to get treated to lunch three or four times a week, huh?"

Kim laughed. "Well, you started it!"

"You damn right I started it, and I'm gonna finish it. Here give me those feet," he demanded as placed them on his lap. Then, he started to massage them.

Kim thought she was in paradise. "Now, that feels nice."

"Have you had dinner?"

"As a matter of fact, I just finished some salad and tilapia. Would you like me to make you some?"

"Aww shoot! You gonna cook for a brother?" He squeezed her foot tightly.

She moaned a bit. She hadn't realized how sore and tired her feet were from rushing back and forth through the offices at the Justice Center all day in her high-heeled sandals. "Sure. There's nothing to whipping up a salad and grilling a couple of pieces of tilapia."

"Well, let me finish your foot massage first. I can't have you in there slaving over a stove with sore feet."

"Where have you been all my life?" Kim moaned again and laid back on the sofa, putting one of her white pillows underneath her head.

"So, have you heard from Len?"

"Not this week. Why?"

"I have to stay up-to-date on my competition." James slowly brought her right foot up to his lips and kissed her big toe.

Kim squirmed. "He's no competition for you." But no sooner than those words left her lips, her mind went back to her encounter with Len on the sofa before James walked in on them, and she wondered if James could please her like Len could.

"He does want you, doesn't he?" James began to massage her calf.

"He said he wants to get back together, but he lives in Columbus. That's too far away for me."

"So, that's the only reason you're turning him down? Distance?" He moved up to her thigh. Kim thought that his touch was soothing.

"Are you trying to get me to say something?"

James kissed her knee cap, "I only want you to tell me the truth, Beautiful." He kissed the inside of her thigh.

"What are you doing?" she asked, more because she didn't want to seem easy than any real protest.

"Trying to please you. How am I doing?" He kissed her further down her thigh.

She moaned in anticipation. "You're doing good," she managed to say.

He slid her panties to her ankles and slipped them off and began to kiss her between her legs more passionately than any other man had.

He's much better than Len, she thought as she moaned over and over and immersed herself in the pleasure he gave her.

She felt a twinge of conflict in her heart as she realized that she was about to make love with the brother of the man to whom she knew she was supposed to spend the rest of her life. She wanted to stop him, but she was getting close to an orgasm. She cried out so loud when she came that she was sure everyone in the apartment building had heard her.

"Let's go to your room," he suggested.

She followed willingly as he led the way.

43

Kim tossed and turned as she dreamt about coming into Richard's office, seeing him staring out of the window again. This time, he turned to her, and she saw his face. She placed the file folders on his desk, "Good morning, Lieutenant Kemper."

"Good morning, Ms. Nelson."

"Here are the reports that you need to sign." She pulled the lapels on her black suit jacket, and smoothed her thigh length black skirt.

"So, is that all you have to say to me this morning, Ms. Nelson," he grabbed her by the hand as she tried to leave.

"What else do you want me to say?"

"I want you to say that you want me."

"So, you can remind me how committed you are to your wife again?" Kim jerked away from him, and started for the door again.

"Wait!" Richard called after her.

"Yes, Lieutenant Kemper."

"That won't happen again. I promise."

Kim looked into his eyes. She knew his desire for her was real. She turned and walked back to him, and they kissed—a long, lingering, passionate kiss.

"I'm so sorry," he whispered in her ear.

"Sorry for what?"

"For hurting you. Putting my wife ahead of you."

"That's why I love you so much," Kim told him. She melted into his chest, and slowly loosened his gray tie with splashes of yellow and unbuttoned his yellow shirt.

"You love me?" he asked as he kissed her neck.

"I think I do," she admitted. She unzipped his gray pants.

He knocked all the file folders on the floor along with the picture of Janice and his sons. They crashed onto the floor, and he stared at the picture for a moment. Kim looked over the edge of the desk to see the family picture staring back at him through the cracked glass.

"Are you okay?" She feared that he would tell her once again that he couldn't do this to his wife.

"I need you, Kim," he said.

Kim breathed a sigh of relief, "I need you, too."

She melted at the touch of his hands gliding up her red low-cut blouse, cupping her breasts firmly and pinching her nipples. "So, does that mean you'll give it to me the way I like it."

She winced at the pain in her nipples when he pinched them, but eager to please her boss, she declared, "I'll give it to you any way you want it."

He pushed her down on the desk and dropped his slacks. Then, he raised her skirt and ripped off her underwear.

"Richard!" she screamed. "Wait, take it easy!"

"This is how I like it," he told her. Then, he thrust himself inside her anus as hard as he could.

She screamed out in pain. "You're hurting me, Richard!"

"You want me, don't you?" he whispered as he continued the forceful strokes. "Just relax. You like it rough, don't you?"

"Richard, stop! You're hurting me!"

"If you would stop fighting and relax, you would like it," he whispered. He stopped moving. "Can you relax?"

"Just go slower, please," she begged. Her eyes watered with tears from the pain.

"Okay," he agreed. Then, he stroked her more gently for a few minutes.

It started to feel better, and Kim began to grunt with his movements. "Do you think someone will catch us?" she asked between grunts.

"Most everyone is gone in our department," he told her and he sped up his rhythm.

"Are you sure?" She whimpered as it started to hurt again.

"I'm sure." He thrust harder. "I'm almost there," he assured her.

She moaned louder, and he thrust harder.

"Richard!" she screamed when she thought she couldn't take anymore.

She woke up, and stared into James' angry eyes.

"Are you dreaming about my brother?" he asked.

"Of course, not," Kim answered. She sat up straight.

"Why did you yell out his name?" He sat up straight, too. He grabbed his underwear from the floor and started to get dressed.

"I don't know. I was asleep."

"Well, if it's my brother you want, you're welcome to him!" He slipped his white muscle shirt over his hard muscular body and pulled on his pants. Then, he stormed out of the room, downstairs and out the door.

Kim heard it slam as she sat there in bed, trying to process what had just happened.

44

It was about 1 in the afternoon on the third Saturday in June when Kim walked into Dr. Ball's office in a gray, cotton mini dress. She felt a bit depressed when she took her usual seat on Dr. Ball's sofa.

"Good afternoon, Kim," Dr. Ball said as she rolled her black chair over to Kim with her yellow legal pad and black pen. "Are you ready to explore your dreams some more," she asked. She seemed much more cheerful than usual. Kim wondered why she wore a white tennis outfit instead of her usual business attire.

"I guess," Kim answered her. She didn't feel good about her dream this time. She was angry with Richard for being so rough with her. She had to keep reminding herself that it was just a dream. Richard would never be rough with her in reality. He was a gentleman. He was a family man—a good man.

"Is something wrong, Kim?" Dr. Ball looked sincerely concerned. She stood from her chair and went over to her desk to put the recorder in her drawer. "Oh, and excuse my appearance today. My husband and I are playing tennis after I finish our session."

Kim felt a twinge of jealousy that Dr. Ball had such a normal life and a husband. She glanced at her wedding ring and felt the longing in her heart to know that kind of commitment from a man. "I had another dream about Richard last night," she said.

"Well, that's not unusual, is it?"

"Having the dream isn't unusual, but the dream itself was very unusual."

"How so?" Dr. Ball looked very intrigued, and sat in her chair again, putting her pen to the paper like she was in a race to write Kim's words as quickly as she spat them out.

"He hurt me," Kim whispered, and she began to weep.

Dr. Ball swiveled around in her chair and reached on her desk for a box of tissues. She handed them to Kim. "How did he hurt you?" she asked.

"He was rough with me when we had sex."

"Well, Kim. It was just a dream. No need to get upset. Has he ever been rough with you while you were awake?"

"No."

"Well, see. There's no need to be so upset. Let's explore the meaning of the original dream—the recurring one, and then, if we have time we may explore the one you had last night. But, before we begin, I want to give you a 'dream journal.'" She reached for a purple spiral hardback journal that was positioned next to the wooden owl.

"A dream journal?" Kim patted her eyes with the tissue.

"Yes, in this journal, I want you to write what happens in your dreams, and I want you to take special note about how you feel when you dream, especially when you have dreams like you had last night."

Kim took the journal from Dr. Ball and flipped through the pages. She noticed that the journal had spaces for her to write the date of her dreams, a summary, and then it had questions to answer about the dream.

"Thanks," she told Dr. Ball.

"You're welcome. Now, before we get started, I want you to record as much information about the dream you had last night. I'll make a copy of your notes so we can explore the dream in our next session. It's important to record information about your dreams as soon as possible so that you don't forget anything."

Dr. Ball enjoyed a cup of tea while she allowed Kim time to write her notes about the dream. After about fifteen minutes, she said. "Okay. Let's get started. We said that we would explore the office—the place where the dreams occur, right?"

"Yes," Kim agreed.

"So, tell me what do you see in the office?" Dr. Ball asked.

"Well, I'm always putting files on his desk."

Dr. Ball wrote down the word, 'files.' "Yes, what else?"

"I think I often have papers for him to sign."

"Hmm," Dr. Ball said, noting the detail, and looking reflective. "Do you seem aware that you're his secretary?"

"Aware that I'm his secretary?"

"Yes, are you aware in the dream that you're his secretary?"

"I'm not sure," Kim admitted.

"You will need to increase your awareness of more details when you dream."

"How do I do that?"

"Write down what you want to remember about your dreams before you go to sleep. Focus on it before you go to sleep in some way."

"Can you interpret anything from what I've told you so far?" Kim moved to the edge of her seat.

Dr. Ball leaned back in her chair, "Would you like some tea before I start analyzing your dream? You seem a bit tense. You need to relax."

Kim tensed at Dr. Ball's words. She noticed a purple stress ball on the table next to the sofa.

"I said you need to relax!" Dr. Ball stated in a firm voice.

Tears streamed Kim's face. "Please stop saying that."

"What did I say?" Dr. Ball moved closer and touched Kim's thigh in an effort to comfort her.

"Don't touch me!" she screamed.

"What is it, Kim?" she urged Kim to answer her.

"*He* kept telling me to relax, and hearing you say it just reminded me of the dream."

Dr. Ball got up from her chair and went to make Kim a cup of tea. "Maybe you need to tell me what happened," she said as she handed Kim the tea and took her seat again.

Kim picked up the stress ball and began to squeeze it as she recounted the dream about the rough sex with Richard then waking up to James, who promptly walked out on her when he realized that she'd been dreaming about his brother.

Dr. Ball was quiet as she listened, occasionally writing notes on her legal pad. Finally, she said, "Kim, you have to remember what I told you. Dreams are seldom literal. They are more often symbolic. Now, just because you dreamed that Richard was rough with you in the dream doesn't mean that he's going to be rough with you in reality. The two of you may never have a sexual encounter. The dream might be a warning that your attraction to your boss is dangerous for you."

Kim stopped squeezing the ball and stared at Dr. Ball with intense anger, "Dr. Ball, you will stoop to anything to keep me from being with Richard. What's with you? Why don't you want me to be happy?"

Kim threw the ball against the wall and it bounced off the wall and hit the owl, causing it to tumble over on the floor. Embarrassed and confused, Kim grabbed her purse and stormed out of Dr. Ball's office once again.

45

It was about 4 that same afternoon when Sheila arrived at Kim's apartment.

"Hey, I got here as soon as I could," Sheila said as she walked in the door and took a seat in Kim's white recliner.

"Thanks, I appreciate it." Kim's mood was somber.

"What's wrong?" Sheila asked. "Looks like you've been crying. You're eyes are all red and puffy."

"I made us some chicken alfredo," Kim said to try to change the subject.

"That's sounds great. You need me to help you serve." Sheila got up from her seat on the sofa and followed Kim into the kitchen.

"I don't really need any help," Kim told her. She opened her light brown wood cabinet by its gold handle and pulled out black stoneware dishes on which to serve the pasta dish.

"You may not need any help with the pasta, but you need help with how you're feeling. You seem so upset. What happened?"

"I don't know where to begin," Kim started as tears fell again.

"Well, try the beginning."

Kim filled the two plates with the pasta, added garlic bread sticks, and placed the plates on the kitchen table. She took a seat at the table with Sheila after she poured them both a glass of lemonade and set Parmesan cheese on the table. "I don't know if I'm upset about the dream, James, or my therapy session today."

"James? What happened with James?" Sheila scooted her chair closer to Kim as she took a big bite of the pasta.

"James came over last night, and we made love for the first time," Kim admitted.

"Well, I'm happy to hear that!" Sheila announced and ate some more pasta. "So, did you like it?"

"It was great," Kim said in a soft voice.

"No problem there." Sheila sprinkled her pasta with some cheese and bit one of the breadsticks.

"I had another dream about Richard, and I called out his name in my sleep." Kim took a small bite of her breadstick.

"Oh, Lord! And he heard you, didn't he?"

"He did."

"So, what happened?"

"He got mad and left."

"Well, I can't blame him! You need to stop pining after his married brother. I wish you would let it go!"

"Look, Sheila. I'm not in the mood for one of your sermons!"

"I don't care! I'm not going to stand by and let you ruin someone's marriage!"

"I thought you were supposed to be my friend!"

"I am your friend. A friend has to tell you the truth, and you need to be ashamed of yourself, lusting after that man. He's married! I hate women like you!"

"You hate me?" Kim stood to her feet.

The women were silent for several moments.

"I don't hate you. I hate what you're doing." Sheila said in a soft, quiet voice. "You got any of that Seven Daughters?"

"I don't know if I want share any of it with you."

"Kim, I've never told you this, but when Damon cheated on me. The affair resulted in a pregnancy."

"A pregnancy?"

"Yeah! Bitch was calling my house, bragging about it and everything!" Sheila took another bite of her pasta. "You know, Damon and I haven't been able to conceive."

Kim went to the refrigerator and pulled out a bottle of Seven Daughters Moscato and poured two glasses. "No. I didn't know, Sheila."

"I know you didn't know. I didn't want anyone to know." Tears welled up in her eyes.

Kim went to the living room to get her box of tissues. She handed it to Sheila. "So, what happened?"

"Damon was talking divorce. Said he loved her."

"Oh, no!" Kim cupped her mouth and took a seat at her kitchen table across from Sheila.

"Oh, yes," Sheila nodded, and tears streamed faster than she could wipe them away.

"I'm so sorry you had to go through that, Sheila."

"You ain't no sorrier than I was." She gulped down the whole glass of wine in a single swallow.

"Well, obviously, you guys worked it out." Kim sipped her wine.

"We did. It took prayer, counseling, and a whole lot of forgiveness," Sheila admitted. She looked up, "And of course, it didn't hurt that the baby was stillborn."

"Oh my goodness," Kim gasped.

"I don't wish that on any woman. I don't want you to cause Mrs. Kemper that much pain. She loves her husband, and Kim, he *does* love her. If you continue in this obsession with him, someone is going to be seriously hurt. Please. I'm begging you. Let it go."

"I had a bad dream about Richard last night," Kim whispered.

"A bad dream?"

"He was rough with me. He hurt me."

"So, does that change how you feel about him now?"

"I'm not sure. Dr. Ball said that the dream—the nightmare, may have been a warning that getting involved with him would be dangerous."

"Kim, I know it would be dangerous and very painful for everyone involved. Let it go. I'm begging you."

Kim took another bite of her pasta as she contemplated her friend's words in silence.

46

On a Saturday evening in late June, Richard came home from playing basketball with his brothers and went to his bedroom to find his wife throwing a minor tantrum. She was opening his drawers and throwing all of his clothes on the floor, fussing and cussing to herself.

"Janice! Baby, what's wrong?" he asked, approaching her cautiously.

She stopped moving for a moment. She wore a red sundress. Her hair was a bit disheveled and her dark skin was moist with sweat. Richard never remembered seeing her in red before, and it didn't look sexy on her like it did on most women, especially Kim. It seemed to yell with hostility just as her words did when she answered, "You're what's wrong!" glaring at him with more anger than he'd ever seen in her eyes before.

"What did I do?" He wanted to embrace her, but he was sure that she would hit him.

She did hit him with a crumpled piece of paper right in his left eye. The paper fell to the floor, and he picked it up. He opened it. It was the receipt from the Embassy Suites Hotel in Beachwood.

"Janice, I can explain," he said immediately.

"Can you?" she asked with sarcasm as she continued to throw his clothes out of drawers.

"I just went there to get some rest. I'm having trouble sleeping with the way things have been between us lately."

"Really, Rich. You expect me to believe that?"

"It's the truth, Janice!"

"Don't do that, Rich. Please don't do that!" She headed to their walk-in closet and began to throw his clothes from the hangers onto the floor.

"Then, you stop throwing my clothes around!" he demanded.

Janice stopped throwing the clothes and looked Richard in the eye. "So, you're saying if I stop throwing the clothes, you're going to admit the truth?"

"Okay, Janice." Richard walked over to their queen-sized bed covered with the yellow, gray and white comforter and sat on the edge of it.

"Who is she?" Janice asked.

"Kim Nelson, my secretary."

"How long? How often?"

"We kissed at the picnic, and we made love. I mean we had sex once."

"You said what you meant. You made love to her! You love her?"

"Of course, I don't love her. I love you!"

Janice began to pick up the clothes and stuff them into a duffle bag. "You need to get the hell out of here," she declared.

"We can work this out, Janice. I tried to remain faithful, but something weird kept happening to me."

"Something weird? Rich, you need to leave. I can't even look at you right now."

"Well, you know I got that detail assignment in Detroit. Let's say I go complete that, and then, when I get back we can revisit this. I don't want to lose you, Janice. I really regret sleeping with her."

Janice threw the black duffle bag into Richard's face. He caught it. She turned away from him and started to cry, "Rich, why did you do it, then?"

"I just couldn't help myself, Janice. But, I promise you the moment it was over, I regretted it deeply. I never want to be with her again."

"Yeah, but do you want to be with me? You don't even desire me anymore, Rich! You think I haven't noticed that!"

Richard got up from the bed, dropped the duffle bag on the floor, and moved close to Janice from behind. "I'm sorry about that, Janice. All I know is I love you, and I don't want to lose you. I don't want to lose us—our family, our life. Please don't throw it away. Just give things a little time. I know the desire will return."

"Could you just leave? I don't want the boys to see how upset I am with you until I've had some time to think about all of this."

"Okay. I'll leave, but I'll be back next Friday, and we'll work this out."

"Whatever."

47

On Monday morning around 10 am, Richard stared out of the window of a Comfort Inn in Detroit, Michigan as his brother, Junie tapped away on the keys of his laptop.

"You come up with anything?" he asked his brother. He left the window and plopped down on one of the double beds and stared at the ceiling.

"This is definitely the place where she met him that day." Junie assured Richard.

"Were you able to pull up any records about what time she usually comes here to meet with the men?" Richard got up from the bed and went over to the window again where he could watch for their suspect to arrive.

"It's usually around noon," Junie shared. "Her cell phone records indicate that she comes here every day at noon during the week. It must be her lunch break from work or something."

"Or the lunch break for the men she's services," Richard interjected. He searched for his 2014 Chevy Impala as he stood in the window.

Junie stopped keying for a few seconds. "You okay, Man?" he asked.

"Amazing," Richard said as he turned away from the window to look at his brother.

"What?" Junie asked.

"The lengths that men will go to in order to get some good sex."

"Well, at least he wasn't stupid enough to get the room with his own credit card. He let her get the room." Junie laughed.

"You think that's funny," Richard said in a stern voice.

"Now, don't get no attitude with me 'cause you messed up your marriage," Junie warned him.

"Well, you're my brother, Man. How can you make jokes about my pain?"

"Man, how long you've been knowing me?"

"All my life," Richard answered.

"Then, you should know by now that this is what I do! And I got a whole lot more jokes where that one came from," he said as he continued to stare into the screen of his laptop, pecking the keys with the quickness of the Road Runner.

Richard plopped down on the bed hard, and then, he leaned back and resumed his gaze into the ceiling something about the stucco design seem to hypnotize him and soothe the pain he felt about the mess his life had become. "I really messed up this time, Junie," he admitted.

"I'll say you did."

"How's things going with Catherine?" Richard asked, picking up the phone to call Room Service.

"She's okay. It's her father that's giving me the blues," Junie answered. Then, he jumped up and brought the laptop over to Richard. "Is this the information you need?"

"Yes, Room Service? Can you bring a couple of your breakfast specials up to room 713? Thanks." Richard sat up and stared into the computer screen his brother had shoved into his face.

"The cell phone records show that he was here around noon the day he was murdered. But check this out, his wife's cell phone records show that she was here, too."

"It looks like she knew about his mistress. And we're certain that the mistress is always here at noon, right?"

Junie nodded to affirm his brother's question and rushed back to his seat at the desk. "I'm double-checking that now."

"So, what are you going to do about Catherine's father?" Richard laid on the bed again and continued to stare at the ceiling.

"Nothing I can do. Hell, if bringing home ninety grand a year doesn't convince him that I can take care of his daughter, I don't know what else I can do."

"I know that's right, Man. I'm proud of you, Junie. You've done well, and I don't think I'd be able to crack this murder case by Friday and get back home to my family if it weren't for you." Richard pulled a Ziploc bag containing a piece of jewelry from his pocket and held it up in the air. "Once I turn in the file on these cell phone records and catch this woman coming back to try to find this earring, this investigation is a slam dunk for Detroit's prosecutor's office."

"If these cell phone records are any indication of her routine, she should be here in about a couple of hours. In the meantime, I'm ready for that breakfast you just ordered." Junie got up from his seat and started to rub his belly. "So, do you think Janice will take you back when you get home?"

"I can only hope," Richard got up from the bed and began to pace the floor.

Junie sat down again and resumed clicking keys on his laptop as if he'd just come up with a new idea.

After several minutes, someone from Room Service knocked with their breakfast. Richard opened the door, tipped the server, and brought in the cart. He and Junie ate quickly. Junie ate while still perusing cell phone records and other digital files to help Richard with his case.

Richard ate while pacing and occasionally looking out of the window for his suspect to arrive.

"So, who's this girl that turned your eye from the love of your life?" Junie asked, gulping down a glass of orange juice.

"Her name is Kim Nelson." He pulled out his phone to show Junie a picture.

"Damn! I see what you mean. She's fine in that red! You know that's my favorite color, and she's wearing the hell out of it!"

"Seems like the Kemper men have very similar taste," Richard said in a solemn tone.

"Well, we all came from the same place. What's wrong with that?"

"Janice ain't the only one I'm in trouble with when I get home," Richard confessed.

"What you talking about?" Junie put down the slice of bacon he was eating, and he stopped keying to give Richard his undivided attention.

"James is dating her."

Junie jumped up from his seat and stared Richard down, "You mean to tell me you slept with our brother's girl! Are you crazy?"

"I tried to—"

"Man, I ain't trying to hear that mess! You should be ashamed of yourself."

"Junie, I'm catching enough hell without you dumping on me, too. I don't know what got into me, but I couldn't stop thinking about her. I can't even make love to Janice anymore. She was all I could think about. I never meant to hurt Janice or James. I'll make it right. I'll find a way."

"You better!" Junie slammed the top of his laptop down and turned his back to Richard, pacing the floor and huffing with anger. After a few moments when he regained his composure, he sat down again, reopened his laptop and started to work again, stuffing his mouth with toast, bacon, eggs, toast and gulps of orange juice—all while still keying.

Richard relaxed when Junie was back at work, and he decided to look out of the window again. He munched on a piece of crispy bacon, but he didn't have much of an appetite. "Hey! She's early! Call Johnson on his cell phone. He's working out in the fitness room. Tell him to meet me on the second floor, Room 201." He slipped on his gun holster and ran out of the door.

48

It was about 7 on Friday evening when Richard returned home to face the music with his wife. He found her sitting at the dining room table alone with a plate of fried perch and French fries. He took in a deep breath and looked in the kitchen cabinets for some Lysol to get rid of the fish smell. He knew that Janice had fried the fish to agitate him. As he sprayed the Lysol, he looked at her again. She had on a green sundress that contrasted nicely with her dark skin, and her shoulder length black hair was full of body and laid on the nape of her neck like silk. She looked beautiful and elegant—the mother of his boys. He loved her. He didn't understand why he'd risked losing her for a woman that his brother wanted. He'd never been so reckless in all his life.

As he walked into the dining room to join her, he felt a bit of peace from the peach-colored walls and other warm tones that characterized their home. The dining room is where they settled a lot of family matters, discussed several rules and goals with their boys and shared romantic candlelight dinners on evenings when they were alone. What had he done? He couldn't help but ask himself that over and over in his mind.

"Hi," he said as he took a seat at the table.

"Hello." She rolled her eyes and slid a stack of papers over to him.

"What's this?"

"Divorce papers."

"Janice, don't do this. We haven't even talked about this. What about our boys? What about our life? You can't just throw it all away!"

"Let's get one thing straight, Rich. I didn't throw anything away. You threw it all away when you set out to sleep with that woman. You didn't give me or our boys a second thought when you screwed her!"

"Baby, I'm so sorry, but just give it some time. I'll make it right. I promise. Just give me a chance."

"And by the way, your brother is looking for you?"

"Who? Anthony?"

"You wish it were Anthony."

Janice got up from the table and took her plate to the kitchen.

Richard followed her. "What do you mean by that?"

"I mean that James is looking for you, and I think you need to go see what he wants. I don't want all that drama in my house."

"What do you mean, Janice? This is my house, too."

"Not for long."

"Janice, please. Don't do this."

Janice turned and pushed Richard as hard as she could. She pounded her fists in his chest with as much force as she could muster. "Stop acting like this is my fault! You did this Richard! You did this!"

Richard backed away, holding his hands up to protect himself from Janice's punches. "You're right. You're right. What do you want me to do?"

"I want you to leave. Go see your brother. Get the rest of your things and leave me alone."

"You're not going to even let me say good-bye to the boys?"

"I'll have them call you. Just get out!"

Richard looked at his wife, and he could see the pain in her eyes—the pain he had caused. Now, he had to face his brother. If the way Junie had acted was a slight indication of what he was going to get when he saw James, he already regretted every kiss he'd shared with Kim, every touch, and even the sex—it just wasn't worth it. How he wished that he'd known how much having sex with his secretary was so not worth the pain he was causing his wife, his sons, and his brothers. They all meant so much more to him than that one sexual encounter with her. He moved cautiously around his wife and headed for the door.

49

Richard got to James' apartment at around 8 pm. He took a deep breath and prepared for their confrontation as he rang the buzzer to his apartment. James did not ask who was at the door. He just buzzed Richard in.

When he walked into James' apartment, he was met by a hard punch in the face that caused him to drop to the floor. As he tried to focus, he saw his brother standing over him. He saw James' weights sprawled across the floor. He wondered had James been doing some extra lifting in preparation for his visit. He could hear a sports commentator announcing the Cavs' game, but he couldn't tell who was winning. At this point, he didn't really care a whole lot about the outcome of the game.

He wondered if he should try to say anything to his brother as he lay there quietly contemplating whether he should gather himself and get up off of the floor.

"You just gonna lay there?" James asked him finally.

"Depends," he answered.

"On what?" James paced around him.

"On whether you plan to hit me again." Richard felt his nose. Blood poured.

"So, you just gonna lay there like a punk? You ain't gonna fight me like a man?"

"Man, I ain't trying to fight you. You're my brother."

"Oh, we're too much family to fight, but it's okay for you to screw my girl!"

"It was just one time, James." Richard sat up.

"So, that makes it okay," James kicked Richard in the gut.

He grimaced and held his stomach tight. "Come on, Man. Let's just talk. I'm not your enemy."

"Man, you lucky it's just me whipping your ass. Johnny and Anthony want some of you, too. And Junie called and told me it was all he could do to keep from jumping in your behind. Man, I thought you supposed to be so upstanding! Such the good guy! I told you how I felt about her, and of all of the women in the world, you choose to cheat on your wife with the woman I love!"

"Love?" Richard struggled to sit up again. "Man, you love her?"

"Man, don't try to act like you didn't know how I felt. I've been telling you how serious I am about her for weeks."

"That's just it, James. You've only known this girl for a few weeks, and you're talking love!"

"When it's right, you know it." James stepped over Richard's legs and headed to his kitchen to get a beer out of the refrigerator. Then, he came back into the living room, took a seat on his sofa and resumed watching the Cavs' game.

Richard sat up. He pulled tissue from his pocket to catch the blood that flowed from his nose and mouth.

"James, you know I've been going through a lot at home. Janice and I were having problems. I was on edge. I've been suffering from stress at home and at work. In my right mind, I never would have hurt you or Janice like this. Come on, Man. Forgive me."

"Man, get the hell out of my house!" James turned up his beer bottle and turned his back on his brother.

Richard struggled to get to his feet. He looked at his brother. He was tired. He couldn't believe how unforgiving Janice and James were being.

They were treating him as if he made mistakes all the time—like he'd hurt them over and over again. It infuriated him that they couldn't forgive him for one lapse in judgment, one lapse in character, one mistake.

50

Richard arrived to his room at the Embassy Suites Hotel in Beachwood at around 10 that night. He was exhausted. He had already ordered room service, but he decided to take a hot shower and lay down on the bed. After about thirty minutes, he heard a knock on the door.

He opened it, and Kim Nelson walked in. As she brushed passed him, he took in the scent of the Obsession perfume that filled the air, and he admired the green shorts and matching top she wore, especially when he saw the way her thighs oozed out of the shorts, looking smooth and inviting. He was immediately aroused. The only thing that reminded him that he had a wife was the green that gave him a short flicker in his memory of her in her sundress earlier that evening.

"I'm glad you could come," he told her as she took a seat on the edge of the king-sized bed.

"Well, I can't stay long, but you made it sound urgent."

"I wanted to apologize." He sat beside Kim and stared into her eyes.

"No need," Kim told him. She crossed her legs and leaned back on her hands.

Richard admired her thighs again. He wanted her again. "Yes, there is a need. I had sex with you, and then, I just dismissed you. That wasn't right. It seems that all I've been doing lately is hurting people that I care about."

"You were right, Richard. You're married. What we did was wrong."

"I won't be married much longer," Richard announced. Then, he got up and went over to the counter where he had champagne chilling along with chocolate-covered strawberries. "Can I pour you a glass of champagne?"

"No, thank you." Kim sat up straight and folded her hands in her lap.

"Come on. Join me for just one drink. Please."

Kim smiled. "Okay. Just one."

Richard handed her a glass, and then, he made a toast, "To new beginnings."

"To new beginnings," Kim repeated.

They drank the champagne, and Richard picked up one of the strawberries. "Have one of these," he told her as he guided it to her mouth.

He watched as her cherry glossed lips wrapped around the fruit and sucked it in ever so sensually. "Hmmm," he moaned. "How does it taste?"

"Delicious. I love chocolate-covered strawberries," she admitted. "But, considering the things we did the last time we were together, I'm sure you already know how much I love them."

"I remember," he whispered as he took Kim's hand in his.

Kim looked at him. Then, she touched his face. "Have you been in a fight?"

"The fight of my life," he answered.

"Your face is so bruised. Let me get a towel and some cold water to put on those bruises." She got up and went to the bathroom to wet some face cloths. She returned quickly, grabbed some ice out of the ice bucket that held the chilled bottle of champagne and put some ice chips inside the cloth, and then, she applied it to Richard's face.

"I think it's really over between Janice and me," he said as he let the coolness of the ice pack soothe his bruises.

"What happened?"

"She found out about us."

Kim dabbed his face a little more in other areas where he was bruised. "How?" she asked.

"She found the receipt for this hotel."

"I'm sorry to hear that, Richard. I know how much you love her."

"You say that like you've given up on us." Richard grabbed the ice pack from Kim and looked into her eyes, searching to see if he saw any more longing for him there.

"You told me to give up on us. You said you were committed to your wife."

"Now, I'm telling you that she doesn't want me anymore. Isn't that what you wanted?"

"I want you to want me like I want you."

"I've always wanted you, Kim. That has never been the problem."

"Then, what's the problem?"

"The problem is I have a wife who I have loved since I was a teen. We have three wonderful sons together. I vowed to spend the rest of my life with her, and then, you come along and ruin all of that."

"*I* ruined it." Kim eyes widened in anger.

"You know what I mean. Kim, I've never been so attracted to another woman."

"So, you have feelings for me?"

"Kim, to be honest, I think I still love my wife. I think that I'm going through some sort of mid-life crisis. Nothing like this has ever happened to me before. I want you more than I've ever wanted anyone, but I love my wife more than life itself. Yet, I want you so much that it affects my sexual attraction to my wife. I don't know how I'm supposed to deal with that."

"Do you think you could ever love me the way you love your wife?"

"I have no idea. All I know is I want you more than I want my wife."

"That's not enough for me, Richard."

"That's not enough for me, either. But, I know I need you right now. I'm hurting so bad, and I just don't want to be alone. Can you just stay with me? I promise we will figure out a way to work this out."

"I don't know, Richard. This already seems very unfair to me. It's seems like you just want me to satisfy you again so you can make me leave when it's over."

"I promise. What happened before will not happen again. Just stay with me tonight. Richard turned on some music from his I-pod and Bose Bluetooth speaker. El DeBarge "Lay With You" came on. What else do you have to do? I just left James. He didn't seem like he had any plans to be with you tonight."

"Did he seem like he had plans to be with someone else?"

"Now, I didn't say all that. Don't put words in my mouth. And besides, I don't want to talk about James."

"Who put these bruises on your face?"

"I don't want to talk about that either" He kissed Kim on the cheek and then softly on the lips. "All I want to talk about is how much I need you tonight. Will you stay?"

Kim kissed him back, and they lay on the bed kissing and touching each other. Every touch gave Richard the comfort he needed. Every kiss gave him the confidence he needed. Every time he heard her moan at his touch, he felt his desire for her intensify. He hugged her tightly between kisses and hoped that she would agree to stay with him for the night. Tomorrow, he would have the strength to win back the love of his wife and the respect of his brother.

51

Kim walked into the office and placed file folders on Richard's desk. He was there, standing in the picture window, staring out at the city's skyline.

"What did you see in him?" he asked.

"See in who?"

"My brother."

"I don't know. I liked the way he treated me. He complimented me a lot."

"Did he make you feel like I make you feel?"

"No one makes me feel like you make me feel."

He moved in behind her, removed her black jacket, and let it fall to the floor. Then, he cupped her breasts in his hands. "No one makes me feel like you make me feel."

Kim felt her knees weaken as he slid his hands from her breasts to her back to unzip her red lace dress. It fell to the floor shortly after the black jacket. She leaned over the cherry oak desk.

"Are you sure we should do this here? Someone might catch us."

"Everyone knows that you're going to be my wife. They'll understand." He slid her panties over her hips, down her thighs, and she stepped out of them. She heard him unzip his pants.

Then, she felt him move slowly and gently inside of her. "Are you okay?" he asked.

"Yes, I'm more than okay," she told him as she immersed herself in the pleasure he was giving her.

"You are so beautiful. I love you so much," he whispered.

When Kim woke up, she looked over, and James was asleep beside her. She was in her bedroom, in her bed, and she was with James—not Richard.

He began to stir, and then, he opened his eyes. "Hey," he said when he saw her staring at him.

"Hey," she replied. She ran her fingers through her weaved, wavy black hair.

"What time is it?" he asked. He sat up straight in the bed, looking for a clock.

"It's 9 in the morning." She pointed to her alarm clock on the red lacquer nightstand next to her bed.

"How do you feel?" He gazed at her nervously as if her response held his last breath captive.

"A little groggy. Did I drink too much last night?"

"You might have had a little too much, but I didn't take advantage of you. Just take a peep under the covers. I still have my boxers on."

"The last thing I remember is talking to you on the phone last night, and you said that you forgave me for calling out your brother's name in my sleep."

"Yes, and you invited me over for a night cap, but you weren't quite ready to resume the sexual part of our relationship, and to tell you the truth, neither was I. Before we go any further, I want you to get my brother out of your system. What's with you and him anyway?"

"Nothing. I just keep having these dreams about him. I dreamt about him before I ever met him."

"Are you in love with him?"

"Why?"

"Because I'm starting to fall for you. As a matter of fact, I've already fallen for you. I really want to be with you, Kim. I haven't felt this way about anyone in a long time."

"Well, I do enjoy your company," Kim said as she got out of bed, pulling down her red T-shirt to cover her red panties.

James got up, too. Kim admired his muscular physique. His abdomen rippled with the impression of his rib cage, and his smooth, broad muscular shoulders looked strong and comforting. She remembered how good it felt to sleep in his arms. "What do you want to do for breakfast?"

"I can make us some bacon, eggs and toast," she told him as she peeped out of her bedroom window.

"That sounds great. You want me to do anything?"

"You can keep me company while I cook." She smiled as she watched him pull his jeans up over his underwear.

"Okay. We've discussed my brother," he told her as he followed her to the bathroom to brush her teeth. "But what about this guy, Len? What are we going to do about him?"

"You're really serious about taking our relationship to another level, aren't you?" Kim asked as she spat out toothpaste.

"Girl, I want you to be my wife!" James replied. He grabbed Kim's extra toothbrush and spread toothpaste on it. Kim saw his facial expression in the mirror as they stood side by side. He looked like he wished he could take those words back.

"What's the matter?" she asked as she gargled with Scope. "Did you misspeak?" She laughed with a bit of uneasiness.

He brushed his teeth vigorously, spat out toothpaste and rinsed his mouth with water. After releasing the water, he said, "I just don't want to move too fast for you."

"Are you saying you really want to marry me?"

"Would you consider it if I did?" He gargled with the Scope.

Kim turned on the shower and stepped inside. "You want to join me?"

Without answering James dropped his jeans and his underwear and joined Kim in the shower.

Kim looked down at him. His size was impressive. She turned her back to him to keep from staring, and he moved in close behind her. She could feel him rising up against her.

"I thought we weren't going to do this yet," Kim moaned as she held herself up by holding on to the shower rail.

"We aren't going to do anything you don't want to do, but if you accept my proposal, I think this would be a fitting way to seal the deal, don't you?" He cupped her breasts and kissed her neck as the warm water sprayed their bodies. "Accepting a marriage proposal in the shower can be a symbol of our new start—a cleansing from all the mistakes we've made. You know what I mean?" He kissed her back. Slowly, he knelt in the shower and kissed her thighs. "You want to do this?"

52

Kim almost skipped into Dr. Ball's office that last Saturday afternoon in June around 1 pm for her appointment.

"Good afternoon, Dr. Ball," she said with a smile as she took her usual seat on the sofa.

"Well, hello," Dr. Ball replied. "You seem like you're in a good mood."

"I am," Kim announced.

Dr. Ball grabbed her notepad and pen. "Okay. Well, let's get started. Do you want to talk about what's got you in such a good mood or do you want to continue to explore your recurring dream? Did you have it again?"

"Yes. Last night as a matter of fact." She stared at the ceiling for a few moments. Then, she turned to look at Dr. Bell. "I apologize for storming out of our last session."

"Kim, therapy is hard work. It's painful work. You're certainly not the only patient I've had who has gotten angry with me when they were having a hard time facing their issues. So, your apology is accepted. Now, let's get back to the new dream. Were any of the details different?"

Kim relaxed. "He asked me what I saw in his brother."

"And what was your response?"

"I told him that he complimented me a lot, but he didn't make me feel like he made me feel."

"Is that statement true in reality?" Dr. Ball asked.

"Dr. Ball, James asked me to marry him." Kim sat up and turned to face the therapist. She stared at Dr. Ball for a response.

Dr. Ball got up from her seat and went over to get a drink. Kim thought she was probably going to make tea again, but she went over to a small refrigerator and pulled out a bottle of water.

"Aren't you going to say anything?" Kim asked after a few moments of silence.

"Did you accept his proposal?" she asked as she sat down and took a sip of the water. "I'm sorry," she said before Kim could answer her. "Would you like something to drink?"

"No," Kim told her.

"You told him no or are you saying no to my question about wanting something to drink?"

"Dr. Ball, why do you think that the last dream I had about Richard was more like a nightmare? Why do you think that he was rough with me in that last dream?"

"What type of intercourse was it?"

"What type?"

"Yes. Vaginal? Anal?"

"Anal," Kim admitted, feeling a bit embarrassed.

"Anal sex often represents a need to release something or someone. Does that mean anything to you?"

"Len, maybe?"

"What's going on with Len? He's the guy that you left Columbus to get away from, right?"

"Yes, he came to see me about a week ago."

"And what happened?"

"I came very close to sleeping with him again." Kim got up from her seat and began to pace the floor.

"How close?"

"I let him perform oral sex on me just before I was to meet James for a date."

"Well, I think that if you plan to pursue a relationship with James, you do need to release Len and Richard. Do you think you can do that?"

Kim got up from her seat on the sofa and walked over to the owl that sat on Dr. Ball's desk. She remembered knocking it over with the stress ball in her anger during the last session. She rubbed it as if she were trying to give it comfort from her recent attack, hoping it would give her some wisdom. "Yes. I don't want to see Len anymore. Len was a very good lover, and it felt good to be with him last week."

"But, you're sure you can let go of him, now?"

"Yes, I'm sure." Kim resumed her seat on the black leather sofa and stared at the yellow of the walls.

"What makes you so sure?" Dr. Ball asked her. She put her pen and pad down and looked at Kim as if she were interested in a real conversation instead of words she had to analyze. She drank her water as if she'd been stranded in the desert for a week.

"I'm falling for James. He's amazing."

"Is he? Have you had sex with him?" She sat back in her chair and became clinical again.

"I have, and it was just like I'd always dreamed love-making should be. He was so gentle, assuring and loving. It was just like my dream about Richard."

"Was it?" Dr. Ball asked as she put down her pad and pen and stood to her feet again. She walked over to the counter to throw away her empty water bottle.

"It was," Kim said. She felt a little unhinged by Dr. Ball's movements. She wished that she would stay in her seat. She laid down on the sofa and stared at the ceiling.

"Was there anything in particular other than Richard standing at the window that stood out to you?" Now, Dr. Ball paced the floor.

Kim closed her eyes, still trying to block out her movements. "This morning I took a shower with James, and he cupped my breasts with his hands from behind. It reminded me of the dream I have about Richard in his office. He always moves up to me from behind and cups my breasts in his hand."

Dr. Ball went to her desk and retrieved her electronic tablet from a drawer. She looked as if she were doing an Internet search. "Just what I thought," she said more to herself than to Kim.

"What?" Kim asked, opening her eyes and straining to turn her neck in order to see what Dr. Ball was doing.

"Sometimes if there is a focus on breasts in a dream, it signifies a need for maternal nurturing. When was the last time you talked with your mother?"

Kim let her head fall back down on the arm of the sofa. "I don't think I've talked to her since the week I moved here. I've been so busy. I usually talk to her every day."

"What do you think she would think about all this?"

"You know to be honest, Dr. Ball. I love my mother, but I would never take advice from my mother about men."

"Why is that?"

Kim sat up and looked Dr. Ball in the eyes. "My mother allowed my father to run around on her, and when he got tired of being out in the streets with God knows how many other women, my mother would just accept him back."

"Have you ever shared your feelings about this with your mother?"

"No. I don't want to embarrass her."

"Well, give it some thought. It might help you break some of your own bad habits with regard to dating men."

"I'd rather focus on my dreams about Richard," Kim said in a flippant tone. She didn't believe she had any bad habits when it came to dating men—just bad luck.

Dr. Ball rolled her eyes in exasperation, returned to her seat, crossed her legs, clicked her pen and repositioned her pad on her lap. "Okay, let's do that. Did you see Richard's face in your dream when he was rough with you?"

"Yes. It was definitely him," Kim replied. She got up from the sofa and walked behind Dr. Ball's desk. Then, she gave her a look as if to ask: *Is it okay if I sit here?*

Dr. Ball nodded in affirmation. "Did you see Richard's face in all the other dreams?"

Kim let the memories of the dreams flow through her mind as she took a seat in Dr. Ball's chair. She remembered walking into Richard's office, and seeing a man standing in the big picture window. She could not see his face. She remembered him cupping her breasts, but she did not see his face. She remembered him penetrating her from behind, but she could not see his face.

"No, I never saw his face," she answered after several moments.

She felt James making love to her in the shower that morning. That was the closest feeling to the feeling of the dream she'd ever experienced. "Dr. Ball, is it possible that even though the dream took place in Richard's office that I could have been dreaming about another man?"

"It's your dream. You could have been dreaming about anyone," Dr. Ball told her as she took her seat again. "Do you think that you were dreaming about someone else?

"I think I've been dreaming about Richard's brother, my fiancé, James Kemper."

53

Later that afternoon, at around 4 pm, Kim returned to her apartment, excited about her discovery that she had been dreaming about James all this time and thinking it was Richard. She threw her keys on the kitchen table and plopped on the living room sofa, turned on some Jeffrey Osborne. James loved him. She played the track, "Share My Love," as she dialed Len's number on her landline.

"Hey, Kim," he said as if he were happy to hear from her.

"Hi, Len. How are you?" She kicked off her white sandals that matched her white sundress, and laid back on her white throw pillows that decorated her red leather sofa.

"I'm much better now that I hear your voice. My divorce will be final soon, and I've been putting in job applications online for a position in Cleveland like crazy. I don't know how I'll adjust to being two hours away from my kids, but I'll only get them every other weekend anyway once the custody agreement is settled."

"Len. I have to admit that all that sounds great, but it's too little, too late."

"Why? Because of that James guy that's been hanging around you?"

"He asked me to marry him, and I said yes."

"You've gotta be kidding me, Kim. How long have you known this guy—a few weeks?"

"I know he's never lied to me! He's not involved with anyone else! He loves me! He wants to marry me!" Kim sat up, angry with herself that she felt the need to defend her decision to Len, of all people.

"Kim, you're making a serious mistake."

"Like the mistake I made when I trusted you?"

"How many times do I have to apologize for that?"

"You don't have to apologize for it ever again! No more apologies are necessary. I've moved on, and I suggest you do the same." She walked into the kitchen and took out some leftover spaghetti to have for dinner.

"It didn't seem as if you had moved on when I was kissing you between your legs last week!"

Kim didn't respond. She tried not to imagine his visit last week. She felt ashamed that she had succumbed to his advances. She tried to justify it in her mind by telling herself that she didn't know how she felt about James then.

"I love you, Kim." Len told her in a soft voice. "You know how much, don't you? Remember how good I made you feel when I was there. Just think about it for a minute."

The last thing Kim wanted to think about was that encounter. "Len, don't go there," she insisted.

"Does he know that you were about to make love to me before he walked into your apartment that day?"

"Are you threatening to tell him?" Kim started to cut tomatoes and cucumbers for a salad to go with the spaghetti. She held the cucumber in her hand for several moments before she could bring herself to cut it. The size of it reminded her of James.

"I'm just saying that you need to think about this. How ready can you be to marry this guy when just last week you were feeling me like nobody's business?"

"I was having a moment," Kim argued. She looked at the cucumber again. She began to peel it gently.

"And what a moment it was. Remember how I kissed your thighs?"

"Len, stop it! I'm not about to go down memory lane with you."

"See me one more time before you marry him. When do you guys plan to get married?"

"We haven't set a date." She stopped peeling the cucumber to slice and dice the tomatoes instead. She poured lettuce from a bag into a big bowl and spooned the diced tomatoes on top of the lettuce.

"So, you'll see me one more time?"

Kim looked at the cucumber again. Now that she had finished peeling it, it felt wet and slippery in her hands. She couldn't help but remember her encounter with James in the shower. She moaned at the thought of how he'd penetrated her from behind as the water sprayed against their bodies.

"Are you thinking about how good it felt?" Len whispered.

"Yes," Kim admitted. She couldn't bring herself to cut the cucumber. She sprinkled the lettuce and tomatoes with shredded cheese and cracked a couple of boiled eggs.

"Can you feel my lips on your thighs?" he asked.

Kim imagined how James had knelt on the floor of the shower, kissing and licking her thighs from behind. Her knees buckled. "Yes," she moaned.

"I wish I were there with you, Baby. I'd make love to you right now. Would you like that? I can be there in a couple of hours. Do you want me to come see you, Baby?"

Kim remembered how they had continued their love-making on her bed when they got out of the shower. He had brought her to a climax three times. *Damn! I wish he was here right now,* she thought. Len was making her so hot with all this talk about making love. "Yes!" she moaned as she realized that she had stopped preparing the salad and was pleasuring herself on the kitchen floor.

"Okay, Baby. I'm on my way," Len told her.

"No! It's over, Len. There's no point."

"Baby, how can you say that? You're over there moaning and groaning like you're going to burst if I don't get to you in the next two minutes!"

"Okay. So, you turn me on. There's more to a relationship than sex, James. I mean Len."

"Did you just call me James?"

"Well, don't get all bent out of shape about it!" Kim went to the kitchen sink to wash her hands. "James is my fiancé. That's who I should be talking to like this—not you!"

"But does James turn you on like I do?"

Kim picked up the cucumber, stroked it again, felt its wetness, its hardness and its size. Then she said, "He turns me on much more than you do!" Then, she hung up the phone, sliced and diced the cucumber, put it in her salad and sat down at the table to enjoy her dinner.

54

James had told her that he wouldn't be back to see her this evening. But, he promised that the next day, he would take her out to a nice restaurant and present her with a proper engagement ring. Kim couldn't wait to tell Sheila. She knew that, if for no other reason, she would be happy that she was finally letting go of Richard, even if she might think like Len and Dr. Ball that marriage was a bit premature. However, Kim was determined that no one would stand in the way of her happiness. James was the man of her dreams figuratively and literally, and she was not about to let him get away.

After she finished her dinner, she decided that she would give him a call to let him know how much she'd enjoyed herself this morning. Then, she would call Sheila to have her over so that she could tell her all about James' proposal, his love-making and her discovery that he was the man in her dreams.

When she called James, he didn't answer. As she prepared to dial Sheila's number, the phone rang before she could dial. It was her mother.

"Hi Mom," she said when she picked up. Then, she started to rinse off her dinner dishes and place them in the dishwasher.

"Hi Sweetheart. I haven't heard from you in a while. Is everything okay?"

Kim turned on the dishwasher. Then, she unwrapped an African violet plant that she'd picked up at Home Depot with some other items she'd bought to add a little spice to her apartment's décor. She usually bought white or red flowers, but she admired the African violets in Dr. Ball's office. Dr. Ball said that they represented wisdom. So, she decided it was time for her to wise up about her choices in men. James was a good choice, and every time she looked at her African violet, she would be reminded of that.

"Everything is fine, Mom. I've just been busy." She placed the African violet in the center of the kitchen table.

"You should never be too busy to keep in touch with your mother."

"I know Mom. How's Keith and Karen? I haven't talked with them either."

"They're okay. The question is how are you? How did things go with Len?"

"I ended things with Len, Mom."

"Good. I didn't want him breaking your heart again."

"Mom, what about your heart?"

"My heart?"

Kim thought about what Dr. Ball had suggested, and she decided that it was time she confronted her mother about her feelings. "Yes, Mom. Are you ever going to start dating again? Dad's been gone for over a year, and you should have started dating again before he even died."

"Kim, your father is the only man for me," she answered after a few moments of silence. Kim could tell that she was crying.

"Mom, I didn't mean to upset you, but how could you be so devoted to him? He cheated on you for years!"

"I loved him, Kim."

"But Mom, how would you feel if Karen or I stayed with a man that cheated on us all the time, or if Keith stayed with a cheating woman? Would you want that for us?"

"You know I always want whatever makes the three of you happy," she said. Her voice quivered a bit.

"Mom, I don't want to hurt your feelings, but you deserve better than a man who did nothing but cheat on you all the time."

After a few moments, Kim heard her mother laugh. Then she said, "Well, Girl. Since you want to go there. You don't know nothing about what that man had between his legs."

"Mom!"

"You started it!"

"Well, I don't want to hear you talk like that."

"Girl, your daddy was a master at love-making. Use to have me climbing the walls, calling my mama, my grandmama, and you know, I called on Jesus! When I think of all that good loving just gone, dead, cold in a box, just brings tears to my eyes!"

"That's why you're crying?" Kim couldn't believe her ears.

"Girl, I tell you. It ain't nothing like a man who know how to give it to you the way you like it. Touch you the right way. Kiss you the right way. Lick you the right way. Girl, what that boy Johnny Gill say, rub you the right way!"

Kim thought her mother was going to start praising God. Even though, she felt uncomfortable with her mother talking about her sex life as if she was one of her girlfriends, she had to admit that her mother was right. Whenever she thought about how James made love to her, she felt like she wanted to go to church and testify! "Mom, it had to be more to your relationship with Dad than sex."

"Oh yes. He provided for me and you kids, too. Brought me his whole paycheck. See, you young women don't understand that you have to give something to get something sometimes. Your mama ain't never been no fool, even though I might have played one from time to time to get what I needed. When your father came home to me, he gave me plenty good loving and all his money. That's what I needed. That's what was important to me. Now, you gotta figure out what's important to you and find you a man that will give you what you need. But, there's another side to that coin. If you want a man to give you what you need, you have to be willing to give him what he needs, and your father needed to be free to do what he wanted whenever he wanted. So, you see, he gave up some things for me, and I gave up some things for him. Yet, in the end, we both got what was most important to us."

Kim would not have imagined in a million years that her mother could give her any worthwhile advice about men, but the words she'd just uttered from her lips gave her freedom in her soul. "Thanks, Mom. I'll keep that in mind," she told her, and then, she hung up the phone.

55

It was about 7 in the evening when Sheila arrived, Kim had their two favorite movies ready with popcorn. "Welcome, my friend," she told her, ushering her with a sweep of her hand toward the living room sofa as if she were royalty.

"So, you look happy," Sheila said.

"For the first time in a long time, I think I am," Kim told her friend as she joined Sheila on her sofa and held up the two movies indicating the question of which they should watch first.

"Toss a coin because you know I want to watch Trading Places!"

"Call it," Kim said, picking up a quarter from the change she had laying on her coffee table.

"Heads," Sheila said as she kicked off her sandals and stood up quickly to smooth her black cotton dress under her butt.

Kim admired how her large breasts filled out the low-cut design. She wished she had more up top. Then, she remembered her morning with James. "I love your breasts," he told her when he cupped them in the shower. She flipped the coin and slapped it against the backside of her palm. "Heads it is!"

Sheila smiled with triumph. "My man, Eddie!"

"He wasn't even all that sexy in Trading Places," Kim complained as she took the DVD out of its case and walked over to the player. "Now, if you want to see some 'got it going on Eddie,' we should watch Boomerang!"

"He was a dog in that movie. I don't like to think of Eddie that way." Sheila grabbed a handful of popcorn.

"You know, I think you need to have a chat with Dr. Ball about that obsession you have with Mr. Eddie Murphy."

"You think?" Sheila laughed and made herself more comfortable on the sofa in anticipation of the movie. "Where's the drinks, Girl?"

"Oh, yeah! I made some of my famous lemonade," Kim announced as she bounced into the kitchen to pour a couple of glasses.

"I wish we were having wine and pizza instead," Sheila called out to Kim.

"Well, it's not too late. I can order some pizza to be delivered, and you know I've always got wine. What you want Moscato or White Zinfandel?"

"I'm so glad you moved to Cleveland, Girl. Let's do some Moscato."

"So, how about we do popcorn and lemonade while we watch Trading Places and wait for the pizza to arrive. Then, when we watch an Officer and a Gentleman, we can have the pizza and wine."

"Sounds like a plan, Girlfriend!" Kim came into the living room with the lemonade, took her seat next to Sheila and pushed play on the DVD player.

Sheila stared at her as the opening credits and scenes played. After a few moments, Kim noticed that Sheila wasn't watching the movie.

"What?" Kim asked.

"You're glowing!"

"Girl, shut up! I'm not glowing."

"Yes, you are. Just look at you. Are you pregnant? Have you been getting your groove on?"

"It's just that things are going really well with James and me."

"It's more than that, Girlfriend." Sheila threw a handful of popcorn in her mouth.

Kim knew that Sheila could sense when she had something to tell her about a man. "We're engaged," Kim blurted out.

Sheila blew the popcorn out of her mouth involuntarily. "Oh my goodness! That's great!" She scrambled on the freshly vacuumed carpet, picking up the popcorn as quickly as possible. Then, she took a big swig of lemonade. Sheila sat close to Kim on the sofa and wrapped her arms around her. "I'm so happy for you, my friend. Hurry up and break out the Moscato! We need to celebrate!"

Kim couldn't believe her ears—no lecture, no concerns. "You don't think we're moving too fast?"

"You can always have a long engagement," Sheila responded.

"I guess we could," Kim responded, giving it some thought. "I told you that Len proposed didn't I?"

"And thank God, you said no!" Sheila looked worried.

"Yes, I said no. You don't have to look so concerned."

"And so what does this mean for your obsession with Richard and that doggone recurring dream you keep going on and on about?"

"Well," Kim started just as her phone rang. "Hold that thought. Let me get this." She looked at the caller ID. It was James. "Hey, Baby."

"Hey, Beautiful. Look, I hate to bother you, but I need you. Can you meet me at University Hospital?"

"Are you okay?"

"It's not me. It's Richard."

"I'll be right there!"

"Sheila, I need you take me to University Hospital. Right now! Let's go!"

56

After Kim left the hotel room, Richard didn't feel any better. He actually felt worse. He didn't feel like living. He felt tired. He didn't know how he'd ever get Janice, James or anyone else in his family to forgive him. He used to find solace at work, but he was tired of all the flack the police department was getting for the breakdown in relations with the Black community. It seemed like every day, his department was under investigation for an excessive force case that had resulted in the murder of a Black person. Heads would have to roll if this bad publicity against the police department continued. It helped some that the high profile cases were being turned over to outside departments, but what if his department messed up on one of the smaller investigations, and then, *it* got blown out of proportion.

Richard opened the bottle of prescription pain killers he had for his headaches. *I should just take all of these,* he thought. What else do I have to live for? No wife. No family. No career. It was morning, but the curtains in the hotel room were closed, and the room was dark and gloomy.

He opened the curtains just enough for him to look out. All he could see was the parking lot. He stared at the cars, each of them seeming to remind him of a murder investigation when he accompanied the forensics unit and instructed them to dust a car for prints or lift forensic evidence from the fabric of seats, his detectives collecting items and placing them in Ziploc bags. He found his black 2014 Chevy Impala among the neat lines of parked cars and wondered what evidence they would secure when they found him dead in it. He looked at his pill bottle again and thought, *they will find this bottle—this empty bottle and rule my death a suicide.*

He wondered if Janice would wish that she'd forgiven him. He imagined that his brothers would struggle with their love for him and their disappointment in him. He pondered what his funeral service would be like. *Who would eulogize him? Who would raise his boys? I have to try one more time* he convinced himself.

He searched his clothes for his cell phone. "Janice?" he said when he heard her voice on the other end.

"Rich, I don't want to talk to you right now."

He thought that was what she'd say. "Baby, I'm miserable without you."

"Really, but not too lonely."

"What?"

"I followed you, Richard. I know you were with her last night. You couldn't even go without her for one night! You lowdown, dirty bastard! I can't believe you would call here acting all remorseful. You son of a…!"

Richard interrupted Janice to say, "I just wanted you to know that I really love you, and I am so sorry for hurting you." Then, he ended the call in the middle of Janice's well-deserved rant. Next, he called James.

"I know you ain't calling my phone!" was the response he got from his brother.

"James. Come on, Man. How long are you gonna stay mad at me?"

"How long are you gonna keep screwing the woman I love claiming you love your wife?"

Richard felt so stupid at that moment. Why did he expect that either of them would forgive him after a day, especially when they both obviously knew that he'd invited Kim back to his bed.

"You really love her, James?"

"I really love her, and you screwed her. Now, what am I supposed to do with that?"

"Look, Man. I promise. I will never touch her again. I just want you to know that I'm sorry, and I need you to forgive me one day. I love you, Bro. And look, if you love her, be with her. Forgive her. We were both in a bad place."

Richard hung up, and left voicemail messages with his other brothers to tell them that he loved them and that he was sorry for disappointing them. He knew what he had to do as he struggled with the decision to end his life. Maybe in time they would forgive him. No. They would never forgive him, and even if they did, they'd never be able to trust him again. He was certain. He looked at the clock on this cell. It was almost 2 p.m. He could hear a couple in the next room making love. He envied them. The night before he felt like he was competing with them. He had Kim crawling the walls, screaming, moaning and groaning. It was much better the second time around, but he knew that his place was with Janice—not Kim. Yet, he could no longer claim his rightful place with her. He'd ruined that for a few orgasms. He'd always considered himself much smarter than that. He was acting like his brother, James, and James for once was being responsible, trying to settle down with one woman. He pushed the thoughts of Kim from his mind along with the sounds of lovemaking in the next room. He went to take a shower. Then, he got dressed and prepared to leave the hotel.

57

⸎

Richard got into his car, turned on the ignition, put the gear in drive, and pulled out of the hotel parking lot. Before driving onto the street, he selected his Marvin Gaye playlist and told himself that as he made his journey to his life's end, he would take a trip down memory lane. He decided to listen to Marvin's "I Want You" album, and the title song played first. He thought about how he and Janice had played that in their hotel room on prom night. He had just discovered a couple of weeks prior to that she was pregnant with Tony.

He headed west to Chagrin Boulevard. He decided he would drive by his old high school, Collinwood, and reminisce for a while. He hit the next track. It was "Come Live with Me, Angel." He chuckled to himself when he remembered how he'd sang that to Janice as they slow danced in their hotel room that night.

He turned right onto Richmond Road. "Are you disappointed about the pregnancy?" he heard Janice ask him as they danced.

"Just because we didn't plan it doesn't mean I have regrets, Janice."

He remembered how he'd spread rose petals all over the bed. They had booked a room with a Jacuzzi.

"James told me that you said you felt trapped."

"He said what!" Just thinking about it made Richard boil with anger again as if it were happening in the moment. James had a lot of nerve being mad at him for sleeping with Kim. He'd almost cost him the wonderful life he'd built with Janice as his wife and the mother of his children.

"He said that you only asked me to marry you because of the baby."

"Janice, you know I proposed because of the baby, but that doesn't mean that I don't love you and want to spend the rest of my life with you.

It just sped things up a bit. I don't feel trapped, and I'll set James straight after this weekend. You better believe that."

He pulled Janice closer. Her fragrance was a sweet-smelling musk oil, and it made him want to melt into her.

"You smell so good," he told her. She wore the most beautiful white and turquoise gown he'd ever seen. The white contrasted with her dark skin like keys on a piano. Harmonious was the best word he could think of to describe her presence when they were alone. Everything about her was in complete harmony with everything about him. He suppressed the memories of all the fights and arguments he and Janice had because she couldn't get pass James telling her that he felt trapped because of her pregnancy. It took him many, many arguments to convince her that he wanted to marry her, first and foremost because he truly loved her.

"After the Dance," came on next. He made a left onto Monticello, and immersed himself in his pleasant memories again. He returned to the vision of Janice in her prom dress—the way she glowed in the candlelight. He remembered how he couldn't wait to get her out of that beautiful gown. He unzipped the gown, and it fell to the floor without much additional effort from him or her. He kissed her neck as he touched every part of her. He could feel the slight bump when he felt her stomach.

"That's my baby in there." He teased her. She giggled. Richard hadn't heard Janice giggle like that in years. When the next song came on, "Feel All My Love Inside," he began to think about how beautiful their lovemaking had been that night. Janice moaned just like the woman on the song.

"You feel so good!" she told him as he filled her. "You think I can get pregnant again?"

Richard laughed as he moved inside of her—gently, rhythmically. He could still remember how soft, warm and wet she felt. He felt like he belonged there. He couldn't imagine making love to any other woman until this year when he seemed to want anybody but her. He could hear her moaning with pleasure as he drove. He wanted to give it to her rough, but he didn't know if she would like that. Plus, he didn't want to hurt the baby, but back then, he was just glad to be with her. The thought of her wetness that night mesmerized him. He almost ran a red light. He hit the brakes hard.

Jarring himself back into the present, he made a right on St. Clair just as "All the Way Around" started to play. He snapped his fingers to the music. When Marvin sang the lyrics about how much he missed the woman he sang about, he dropped his head. "I miss you, Janice," he whispered as he let the music soothe his aching heart. He thought about how ironic it was that Marvin sang about a woman named Janice, too. He started to sing the hook, "If you gotta girl and you want her for your wife, love her all the way around." He couldn't figure out where things got off track.

He approached his old high school and pulled up in the drive. He remembered walking to school with Janice every day. Janice was the only woman he'd ever made love to until Kim. He'd always been satisfied with that. "Since I Had You," played next. Marvin sang about how he'd hadn't been with another woman since he'd been with the woman he sang to, who, according to the lyrics he hadn't seen in a long while.

Maybe that was why he'd stepped out on Janice, since he'd had her, he hadn't been with any other woman. Maybe he needed to satisfy some sort of curiosity that he didn't realize was inside of him. One thing he knew for sure at this moment was that having sex with someone because she's attractive, sexy and seductive was no substitute for making love to a woman who loves you with all of her heart. Having sex with Kim helped him have an orgasm, but beyond that there was nothing else.

He pulled out of the Collinwood parking lot and headed to his office. "Soon I'll Be Loving You Again," played. He wished that were true. He wished that he could be with Janice again. He felt himself rising up at the thought—remembering her in that gown on prom night, the day she told him she was pregnant with his child as they walked to school, making love to her at his parents' house when no one was home. Now, he knew that he had his attraction back for his wife, but it was much, much too late.

58

It was about 4 on that Saturday afternoon when Richard entered his office, he was determined to set his affairs in order. He passed through Kim's office like a blur and unlocked his office door, hit the light switch and headed to his desk. He pulled out his living trust and looked it over. He didn't want to change anything. His life insurance would pay off his mortgage and car note. Janice would get everything. He wouldn't leave a note so his death would be ruled an accidental overdose possibly instead of a suicide.

He went back out into Kim's office and turned on the coffee-maker. He picked up the documents on Kim's desk that she'd left for him to sign and returned to his desk. After he'd signed the documents, he hit the speaker button on his office phone and called his brother, Anthony.

"Hey, Man. What you doing at the office?" he said when he picked up.

"Had a few documents to sign. Listen, Ant. Let's not beat around the bush. I know you're mad at me. I just need to talk to my big brother."

"Man, I don't know if I can talk to you. I'm so disappointed in you."

"I know. I know. I'm disappointed in myself. Do you think it's anyway I can get either one of them to forgive me any time soon?"

"I don't know, Man. How would you feel if James slept with Janice? Maybe that would give you some idea about your chances."

"I guess it won't be any time soon, then. Maybe not at all." Richard picked up the picture of him with Janice and the boys from his desk and stared at it.

"So, I heard Janice served you with divorce papers."

"Yeah. Listen, Man. I really just wanted to tell you how much I appreciate the brother that you've been to me. You were always a good example. You encouraged me and supported me when no one else did, and I love you for it."

"That's what brothers do, Man. I got your message earlier. You almost sound like you're leaving. You know you can't leave, Man, right?"

"I have to do what I have to do, Ant."

"And what's that? You have to stay in your kids' lives no matter what goes down between you and Janice."

Richard put his family picture back in its place on his desk and got up to walk around. He couldn't bear to be reminded of all he had lost anymore. He retrieved the bottle of pain killers from the pocket of his black mesh shorts. "Janice can handle the kids. She doesn't need me."

"Didn't nobody say nothing about Janice! I said you have to be there for the kids. Your boys! Women shouldn't raise boys alone! It takes a man to help a boy become a man."

"Lots of strong women have raised boys to become great men! And you know that."

"Man, I got so many friends, though. Friends that were raised by their mothers who say they have this big hole in their heart for their father. Rich, what's getting into you? You married Janice because you wanted to be a father to your child. What do you think that the only way you can raise a child is as the mother's husband?"

"Listen, Man. I know you're trying to help, but maybe this isn't the best time to have this conversation. I just wanted this talk to be about me and you. I just wanted you to know how much I love and appreciate the brother you've been to me."

"You ain't thinking about doing something crazy, are you, Rich?"

"Hold on a minute," Richard told his brother. Then, he went into Kim's office and turned off the coffee-maker. He poured a cup of the coffee and headed back into his office. "I'm back."

"So. Are you okay?"

"What do you think? My wife of almost twenty years is divorcing me, and my brother hates my guts. As a matter of fact, the lowdown bastard just kicked my ass the other day!"

Richard could hear Anthony laughing.

"You find something funny about how jacked up my life is right now?"

Anthony tried to compose himself. "Hey, it's just that I wish I had been a fly on the wall to see that!" He laughed again.

Richard hit the end call button and threw his cup of coffee against the wall. The ceramic mug broke into about four or five pieces and fell to the floor. Coffee dripped down the yellow walls, making the wall look as if it were crying the tears he felt inside.

He hit the button on his remote control to his stereo, and the Supremes' "I'm Gonna Make You Love Me," blared from the speaker. He could see the phone lighting up, indicating a call was coming in. He knew it was Anthony calling back. *To hell with him*, he thought. He'd said what he wanted to say to him. No need for them to continue their conversation. He knew that Anthony didn't mean any harm by laughing. He'd laughed at his trials and tribulations just the same at one time or another. That's what they did. They laughed at tragedy, and his situation was indeed tragic.

As he listened to Diana Ross make her declarations of love, he wished that he could make Janice love him again. He couldn't believe that he'd gambled with her love and lost—lost big! Only one thing could make this whole situation bearable, and he was determined to go through with it. He stood in his office window and stared out at the Cleveland skyline as he contemplated his fate.

59

It was about 5 pm when Richard reached his house. He pulled in the driveway all the way to the backyard. Janice's van was there, but he was sure that she wouldn't come out. She didn't want to see him. He wasn't planning to go inside. He just wanted to be home where she would find his lifeless body. He hoped that one of his children wouldn't find him first. Janice would find him in his car—probably slumped over the steering wheel. Usually, they would have family movie night since it was Saturday. He had won the choice for this week before Janice found the hotel receipt. He was going to make them watch Shaft in Africa this week, but Janice put an end to all that.

It was approaching evening, and it had been a gloomy, cloudy day. Yet, for some reason the promise of rain had not yet been fulfilled, but you could smell its intended arrival in the air. He had spent the day reminiscing about his life with Janice. Now, he felt it was time that he reflected on his children. He wondered how their lives would turn out. He laughed to himself when Tony told him that he thought his girlfriend, Angie was pregnant when he was nine—just because he had kissed her on the cheek. Nowadays, he worried that his encounters with Angie weren't quite so innocent.

He got out of his car and headed to the deck. He went to the window, which gave him a view of their kitchen. Janice was at the kitchen counter peeling potatoes. She was a wonderful cook. He wondered what she was preparing for dinner. Were they still going to have Family Movie Night? He saw his oldest son, Tony heading toward the door. Quickly, he grabbed a cloth and started to wipe off the patio furniture.

"Hey, Dad!" his son greeted him when he emerged from the house. "I didn't know you were here. Where you been?"

Richard turned to his son and embraced him, "I've been on an out-of-town assignment," he told him. "Your mother didn't tell you?"

"Yeah, about Mom…she's been acting a little weird lately, so I keep my conversations with her to a minimum, if you know what I mean."

Richard smiled, amazed at Tony's maturity. He thought he'd be the *one* to worry about. "I see you got your trumpet. Where you off to?"

"Got an audition for a paying gig! Can you believe it?" Tony pumped his fist in the air in a gesture of triumph.

Richard gave him a high-five. "Of course, I can believe it, Son. You're going to go far with your music. Why don't you play me something before you leave?"

"Really, Dad? I gotta an audition." Tony looked at his father in disbelief.

"Just a few bars." Richard grabbed the water hose, turned it on and sprayed down the furniture. He looked at the gray vinyl siding on the house and felt a little sick at the thought of his plans.

"I don't know why you're wasting time doing that. I know you can tell it's going to rain soon," his son advised him.

"Just wanted to clean it so I can hang out here for a bit. Is that okay with you?"

"Yeah, it's okay with me." Tony hunched his shoulders. "What you want me to play?"

"You know my favorite," Richard told him as he dried off the chaise lounge so he could relax and listen to his son play.

Tony took his trumpet out of its case and after attaching the mouthpiece, he immediately went into "Feels So Good" by Chuck Mangione. Richard laid back on the chaise lounge with his eyes closed and enjoyed his son's rendition of one of his favorite songs. When Tony finished, he heard the applause of a single person. He opened his eyes, and it was his middle son, Sonny.

"I bet you get a lot of girls with that trumpet, don't you, T?"

"Man, ain't nobody out here scouting girls all the time like you. I got a woman. I'm just like Dad. I'm a one-woman man. Right Dad?"

"Yeah, right, Son," he answered, but he couldn't force himself to make those words agree with his soul. He hoped Tony didn't sense it. "My sunshine will chase away these clouds. Ain't that right, Sonny?"

"You know me, Dad. Wherever I go, it's always 70 degrees with no chance of rain!" He licked his lips and flashed his chalk white smile.

"Alright, Dad. I hope you enjoyed your song, but I gotta get out of here. You good?"

"I'm good," Richard told him. "Hey, you're going to get that gig, and I want you to know I'm proud of you. Don't ever give up on your dream." He looked at Tony and held his hand up for a handshake.

"No chance, Dad," Tony replied as he walked off the deck and headed to his destination.

"Hey, what time you coming back?" he asked him, wondering if it were any chance he might be the one to find him.

"I won't be back until late tomorrow. I'm spending the night at Uncle Anthony's. You too, right?" He directed his question to his brother, Sonny.

"Yeah, I'll be there," he said as they dapped each other up.

"So, where are you going, Sunshine?" Richard asked, admiring the love his sons showed for one another.

"Dad! Don't call me that. You might slip up and say it front of one of my honeys," Sonny told him as he picked up his basketball and started to dribble it skillfully. "One of my girls is going with me to pick out a birthday gift for Mom. We're going out to Beachwood Mall."

Richard frowned at hearing 'Beachwood.' It reminded him of how he'd lost Janice. "It's kind of early to shop for a birthday gift for your mom isn't it? I mean her birthday is two months away."

"See, that's the difference between you and me, Dad. I put Mom on a pedestal where she belongs. You treat her like she's ordinary. You guys have been together too long. You're starting to take each other for granted." He twirled the basketball on his index finger.

Richard smiled, both at his son's wisdom and his skill that reminded him of the Harlem Globetrotters. He'd planned to take him to see them the next time they came to the Q Arena. "You're probably right about that, Son."

"Probably?" Sonny smirked. "I *know* I'm right about that. See, Dad. I might have a lot of honeys, but I don't take any of them for granted. Each one of them thinks they're special. That's what women need. I don't know how you got Mom. You ain't got no game!" He playfully punched Richard in the arm and started to leave.

"Buy her something really special, Son." Richard reached for his wallet and pulled out his Visa and threw it to Sonny. "Spare no expense."

Sonny caught the card and looked at his father in disbelief. "Are you serious?"

Richard nodded, and Sonny threw the basketball out into their backyard where the grass was mostly brown and dead, and he ran back to his Dad, knelt to where he was sitting and hugged him tight. "You're the man!"

At that moment, Jr. joined them on the deck. "What's all this hugging about?" he asked, barely looking up from his tablet on which he played a video game.

Richard got up from the chaise and went over to his youngest son, grabbed him and hugged him tight, causing him to drop the tablet. "This is what it's all about!" he said, kissing him on the cheek.

"Dad, you're going to make me lose!" He complained as he bent over to pick up the tablet.

"I'm out!" Sonny declared, and he jogged off the deck and out of sight.

"And I guess you have plans, too. Huh, Mini me?"

"Dad, I'm my own person. It's bad enough you guys call me Junior." His focus was still on his game.

"Well, what would you like to be called?" Richard took his seat again on the chaise lounge.

"RJ, then my name will be just like my best friend, AJ!" He looked up from his game to make his declaration.

"Well, you know what? With logic like that, I think the name deserves some consideration. You should discuss it with your mother."

"Really, Dad?" His words dripped with annoyance. "A name change just doesn't take all that. All you have to do is call me RJ."

"You're right. You're right," Richard tried to appease his son. "It's just that you're going to have to have this conversation with everyone who you want to call you that, and I think your mother would want to know that you don't like what she's been calling you."

"Dad! Don't say it like that. I don't want to hurt Mom's feelings."

Richard didn't want to talk about hurting Janice's feelings. He'd already hurt her more than anyone else could. "Is that where you're going? Over AJ's?"

"Yeah. I'll be back tomorrow, okay? Mom said I could go."

"Yeah, yeah. That's fine."

"Okay. See you later." Junior walked away, still looking down at this video game, and Richard wondered how he was able to see where he was going with his head stuck in the game.

His son was so confident that he'd be here when he got back. Richard reasoned that even if he were alive, his son wouldn't be seeing him anytime soon. He was satisfied that according to each of his son's plans, neither of them would find him after he was gone.

He stood and went over to the window again. Janice was still in the kitchen. She wore pink leggings with a multi-colored blouse that favored pink. He admired how her dark, smooth skin always contrasted so beautifully with so many different colors. In his memory, he heard her say jokingly, "You know Black goes with everything."

He smiled. She was right about that. He pulled his bottle of pills from his black mesh shorts' pocket again. He wished he had asked one of the boys to bring him some bottled water before they left. He had such a hard time swallowing pills at the right dosage, he knew it would be hard to gulp down the 24 capsules remaining in the bottle. He saw his insulated coffee mug sitting on the patio table. He picked it up and ran some water from the water hose in it.

Then, he returned to his car, sat behind the steering wheel, threw the whole bottle of pills into his mouth and washed them down with the water. Next, he turned on his car stereo and let Babyface "Never Keeping Secrets" play until he fell asleep.

60

"He's awake," Richard heard someone say. He felt the presence of several people rushing about around him. His vision was blurry. He could see that there were several people standing around him. He wondered where he was.

"What's going on?" were his first words.

"Hey, how you doing?" he heard his wife say. Her voice sounded sweet, gentle and loving. He could feel her touch on his face. His vision began to clear, and he realized that he was in a hospital, and several people were present, including Janice. He could hear the beeping of a hospital monitor.

"Janice, what are you doing here?" he asked.

"I'm your wife, Silly. Where else would I be?"

"You said you were divorcing me." He tried to sit up, but he felt extremely stiff.

"Richard Kemper! Bite your tongue. Never would I say anything like that!" Janice smiled at him as if she'd never been angry with him. Never told him not to come back to the house. Never gave him those divorce papers. He must have died and gone to some kind of strange heaven.

"Hey, Bro!" Anthony said to him, stepping closer to his bed.

"I thought you were mad at me," Richard struggled to sit up, and he kept blinking his eyes trying to will his vision to become totally clear.

"Mad at you? For what?" His brother looked as if he didn't have a clue as to what he meant.

A white male doctor with white hair in a white lab coat pushed through the crowd that looked as if it were his whole family. "Family," the doctor addressed the crowd. "The nurses and I need to check him out before you bombard him with too much information," he said as he neared Richard's bed.

Everyone filed out of the room, and the doctor looked at Richard's chart for a few seconds before speaking. "Good evening, I'm Dr. Means. How you doing, Sir?" he asked in a hearty voice.

"I don't know. What's going on?" Richard asked again. He guessed that his suicide attempt had failed, but he wanted to hear what determination everyone else had made about the situation.

"Do you know what your name is?"

"It's Richard Kemper."

"Do you know what day it?"

"Is it Saturday?"

"Year?"

"2015."

"Who's the President of the United States?"

"Barack Obama!"

"You seem okay. Do you know today's date?"

"Yes, Doc. I'm fine. It's June 27th. But, how did you save me?"

"You suffered an injury to your head a couple of months ago, and it caused some swelling on your brain. The swelling caused you to experience those headaches you were having. We had to operate to reduce the swelling."

Richard tried to sit up again so that he could continue the conversation. "I have no idea what you're talking about. I meant, what did you do about the pills?" he asked, confused about the doctor's narrative citing headaches and brain surgery.

A black female nurse entered the room. She immediately came to assist Richard with his desire to sit up straight by adjusting his pillows and showing him how to use the control to adjust the position of his bed.

"Pills?" Dr. Means said, looking bewildered and then looking at Richard's chart again.

"You guys gave me some pain killers for the headaches, and I thought maybe I took too many of them." Richard wanted to hide the fact that he'd tried to commit suicide. Obviously, his suicide attempt had failed, and he didn't want to be referred for any psychiatric evaluation.

"We never prescribed any pain killers for you," Dr. Means told him.

"Doc, I've been taking the pain killers for the last month," Richard assured the white man, who in his estimation, wasn't a very good doctor, the way he kept looking at the chart instead of looking at him.

"Mr. Kemper, you've been in this hospital bed for the last month."

"Man, are you some sort of quack? Where did they find you? Where's my regular doctor, Dr. Hansen?"

"Dr. Hansen is your primary physician. I'm your neurologist."

"Neurologist? What the hell do I need a neurologist for?'

"I see you are experiencing a bit of confusion, and that's to be expected. Mr. Kemper, you just woke up from a coma."

"A coma?"

"Yes. Coma patients usually dream a lot, but you seemed to be still living your life while you were asleep. The swelling on your brain caused your headaches, and eventually the swelling caused too much pressure on your brain, and you passed out. After the surgery, you slipped into a coma."

Richard tried to process the doctor's words. He'd been in a coma. "How long have I been in this coma?"

Janice walked in. "Since the annual Memorial Day picnic. Don't you remember? You were having headaches when we got ready to leave the park."

"Janice," Richard looked at her. She looked beautiful. She still wore the pink leggings and multi-colored top that he remembered her wearing when he was gazing at her through the kitchen window from the deck, but did that really happen? If he was in a coma, it couldn't have happened.

"Hey, Baby. Are you feeling any better?"

"I feel okay. So, I've been asleep since the Saturday before Memorial Day?"

"Yes, and I've been here every day—waiting for you to wake up. Everyone's been here, taking turns sitting with you—your brothers, your parents—even your co-workers, especially your new secretary. She's been here almost as much as I have."

"Can I get you anything?" the nurse asked. "My name is Nurse Jenkins."

Richard shook his head to indicate that he didn't want anything. He kept staring at his wife in disbelief. The nurse left the room.

"I'll give you a few minutes with your family," Dr. Means told him. He took one last look at the chart, and he left.

"Where you guys find him?" Richard asked as he realized he was thirsty and started to look around for water.

Janice got up and went over to the counter where there was a pitcher of water and cups. She poured a cup of water and brought it to Richard.

"You know me so well," Richard smiled as he took the cup and drank the water almost in one gulp. He realized that if he had been in the hospital since May, then Janice was not divorcing him. He had not tried to commit suicide. "Where are the boys?"

"They're right outside. Do you want me to get them?"

"No, no." Richard grabbed Janice's hand. He remembered that she loved for them to hold hands. "I'm so happy to see you."

"I'm so happy to see you." she replied.

"How do I look? Do you think I'll scare the boys if they see me like this?"

"Nobody cares how you look, Rich. We're just glad you're still with us. Your whole family is waiting to see you. Your brothers, co-workers, the kids."

"Everybody?" Richard asked. He remembered the kiss he'd shared with his new secretary, Kim Nelson at the picnic. Maybe he'd dreamed about the affair with Kim because, as Janice said, she'd been to visit him so often when he was in the coma.

"Hey, Bro." James said as he entered the room. Kim was with him. They were holding hands. "I tried to wait until they said it was okay for me to come in, but I just couldn't wait to see you."

Richard assumed that James must have continued to see Kim after the picnic. He felt a little uncomfortable seeing her. "Hey, James. It's good to see you." He remembered how James had punched him and said that he didn't want to have anything to do with him anymore. *But that was the dream*, he assured himself.

"Look, who's with me?" James said, pushing Kim in front of him.

She wore a white cotton dress. It was form-fitting, and she looked beautiful in it. "Hi, Ms. Nelson," he said. A flash of him having sex with her in the hotel room sent a chill through him.

"Hi Lieutenant Kemper. It's so good to have you back with us."

"Now, look you two. You're going to have to stop being so formal with this Ms. Nelson and Lieutenant Kemper stuff. This is going to be your sister-in-law, Man!" James said with pride. "Tell him, Baby."

Kim nodded in agreement. "I'm marrying your brother, Lieutenant Kem—, I mean, Richard."

"You guys are getting married?" Richard asked the question as if he hadn't just heard them announce it.

"As soon as you're well enough to be in my wedding!" James blurted out. His enthusiasm filled the room like a big bouquet of balloons. "Kim's father passed away about a year ago, and she wants you to give her away. Ain't that right, Baby?"

Kim smiled and nodded, giving Richard a look that said, *It will be better this way.*

"Give the bride away, huh?" Richard said, looking at his Kim. His look said, *I agree.* But, he still felt he needed time to process their announcement.

James nodded, searching Richard's eyes intensely. Richard kept looking at Janice.

"Can you give us a little more time, James? I think all this is a bit much for him." Janice said after a few uncomfortable seconds of silence.

"Sure," James conceded. He took Kim by the hand, and they left.

Richard reached for Janice's hand again. "Are you going to give her away?" Janice asked.

"You better believe I am," he told her, and he squeezed her hand tight. "I just need to know. Are we good?"

She smiled at him and then she kissed him—a long passionate kiss. He rose to the occasion as she whispered in his ear, "We're good. Are we good?"

He looked down at himself and said, "We're definitely good."

About the Author

Marie Satterwhite was born and raised in Cleveland, Ohio. She's the mother of two (2) wonderful children and grandmother to three (3) grandchildren, who she adores. Her way of life is to love, live, enjoy and laugh often. She is God-fearing and hard-working. She has been in retail management for over thirty (30) years. She has built lifetime relationships with so many people, mostly because of her laugh, humor and overall personality. To know her is to love her. She currently resides in Euclid, Ohio.

Made in the USA
Lexington, KY
20 January 2017